I0742674

CONJURING ZEPHYR

BOOKS BY D. LIEBER

Minte and Magic

The Exiled Otherkin

The Assassin's Legacy

Intended Fates

Intended Bondmates

Intended Strangers

Intended Enemies

Council of Covens

Dancing with Shades

In Search of a Witch's Soul

Also by D. Lieber

Conjuring Zephyr

Once in a Black Moon

A Very Witchy Yuletide

The Treason of Robyn Hood

The Curse of Moonseed Manor

The Goblin King's Mischief

The Winter Sorcerer and the Summer Witch

Bitten by the North Wind

CONJURING ZEPHYR

D. LIEBER

Ink & Magick, LLC
Kenosha, Wisconsin
contact@inkandmagick.com

Hardcover ISBN: 978-1-951239-04-6
Paperback ISBN: 978-1-7328323-5-0
Ebook ISBN: 978-1-7328323-6-7

Cover by GetCovers
Layout by Bryan Donihue, Section 28 Publishing
Edited by A Writer for Life

SPECIAL THANKS

I dedicate this book to Apollo and the muses. Thank you for answering my call.

I would like to thank all of the people who lent me their expertise and their patient ears. Thank you John, Debbie, Mary, Laura, Zech, Michelle, Mom, Amy, Chris, and Brandon.

CHAPTER 1

I first saw the uniforms while visiting Capital Art Museum on a school trip. *But are my cloth manipulation skills good enough to pass muster? I guess I will find out.* Straightening my spine, I marched toward the imposing Student Hall.

My boy-crazy best friend, Patti, coached me on how to walk like a man for weeks. Patti would know. All she does is watch men. She wasn't convinced I could get away with my scheme. She, like everyone else, was convinced there were fundamental differences between men and women that were easily spotted. That didn't stop her from helping me prepare for all foreseeable contingencies.

Student Hall loomed over me as I stepped into the lobby. Students rushed around getting ready for the semester to start.

A large display gave instructions to prepare for new student orientation. "Welcome New Students!" it proclaimed in big, bold letters. My first task was to determine what dorm room I was assigned. Following the arrows to the left, I found a bored looking second-year checking a list and handing out dorm entry chips.

"Name?" he asked me, without looking up from the list. *My first test.*

"Kie Stephenson," I replied, lowering my voice slightly. His eyes flicked to my face, and I resisted the urge to squirm. I stilled my body and smoothed my expression, trying to seem unconcerned.

"Elemental Dorm, fourth floor, east block, room two." He handed me a chip, then waved me away, pointing at a stack of campus maps on the table beside him.

I snatched one and shoved my nose into it, using it as a shield. A quick peek showed me he was already helping another student. I let out the breath I hadn't realized I was holding.

Once I located my dorm on the map, I left Student Hall and noticed a slight boy with blond hair struggling with luggage.

"Do you need help?" I asked him.

He squeaked, clearly startled, and dropped the suitcase. Big blue eyes met mine as he stuttered. "I-I-if you...d-d-don't mind."

I smiled reassuringly. "I'm Kie," I said, holding out my hand.

"Leif," he said, shaking it. He exhaled in relief and returned my smile weakly.

"Where are you headed, Leif?"

"Elemental Dorm, first floor."

"All right, I'm going to Elemental Dorm too. Let me help you," I said, grabbing his dropped case.

"Thanks." He looked tired.

After walking a short while, I asked, "Why didn't you leave the case with the valet?"

Leif reddened and replied in a quiet voice, "My father was watching." My confused expression must have forced him to continue, but he was clearly uncomfortable. "He doesn't think I am strong enough to be an elemental, so he always makes me carry everything."

Leif looked so dejected, I had to save him. "My parents don't live in Capital. I made the journey with friends."

"Oh?" he asked, brightening at the change of subject.

"I'm from the rim. It took me three days to get here by train."

"I've never met someone from the rim before," he said in awe.

Before he could ask any questions, there was a loud crash and someone shouted.

A dark-haired first-year hovered above Elemental Dorm, throwing whirlwinds at the source of the shouting. Another dark-haired first-year stood behind a rock wall, protecting himself from the wind.

"Stop it, Flynn," the boy on the ground yelled. "I am not fixing that window."

Flynn laughed and stuck out his tongue.

A flare of fire forced everyone's attention to the dorm's front door. "Enough," the source of the flame, an annoyed fourth-year, ordered.

Flynn landed immediately, and the other dark-haired boy crumbled his wall.

"Reid, what happened?" The upperclassman demanded an explanation.

Upon closer inspection, the two boys causing the ruckus were clearly twins. Their faces were identical, though their builds were a bit different. They were both the same tall height, but Reid was more muscular, probably because he was an earth user while Flynn was an air user.

Reid hesitated to answer the upperclassman, not wanting to get his brother in trouble.

"The craziest thing, Dorm Leader," Flynn said, drawing the fourth-year's attention to him. "It was a phoenix. I have never seen one so big," he fabricated convincingly.

The Dorm Leader harrumphed and turned to Reid, who avoided eye contact and ducked his head. "Fix it," he said and strode inside.

Flynn and Reid exhaled in sync, then turned to each other. Flynn grinned, and Reid rolled his eyes, then walked to the broken window. Flynn noticed Leif and me. He looked at our ties and yelled, "Hey, fellow newbies," waving his arm in a wide arc as if we needed help seeing him.

Leif and I timidly waved back, unsure but not wanting to be unfriendly. Flynn closed the distance between us.

"Flynn Williams, here to make life more interesting. That's my brother, Reid," he said, grinning and jabbing his thumb over his shoulder. Reid nodded in our direction.

"I'm Kie, and this is Leif," I replied.

Flynn's gaze slid over me intently. As soon as I noticed, it was gone. *Paranoia will make you look more suspicious, Kai.* I straightened my spine.

"What floors?" Flynn asked.

"Fourth for me and first for Leif," I replied.

"Air and earth, huh? Us too," Flynn grinned. "But you already knew that. Leave that case for the staff, and I will show you around." He motioned for me to follow and pointed Leif toward Reid.

"Thanks," I responded.

As I took a step forward, Leif grabbed my elbow to stop me. I met his nervous eyes and was taken aback. *So much like Toby: fragile and looking to me for reassurance.* I squeezed his hand and whispered, "Don't worry. I'm sure Reid will take care of you. I will see you at dinner, okay?"

Reid reconstructed the broken glass, and I watched, impressed that his earth elemental skills were already so developed for a first year. When he had completed his task, he moved toward us. He nodded to Leif, "East block, right? Which room?" Reid's distraction had Leif fumbling for his chip.

I headed into Elemental Dorm in search of Flynn, who had gone ahead, and entered a large common area. Couches, chairs, and tables were arranged arbitrarily around the room. On the far side, a staircase spiraled up and out of sight.

Flynn lounged on a couch, feet up, appearing relaxed. He peeked at me under gently-closed lids. With a flourish and a well-controlled wind, he was standing in front of me, smirking. *These twins are pretty advanced for first-years.*

"The stairs lead to the other three floors. Past them is the dining room. There are four blocks of dorm rooms on each floor, and each block houses eight students. The second floor has an open room for meetings or practice or whatever. The laundry room is on the third floor. What room are you in?"

"Room two."

A mischievous grin, which I realized was his default expression, spread slowly across his face. "Let's head up then, Roomie."

He started up the spiral staircase, and I followed wondering what would result from this unexpected turn.

In the fourth-floor common area, we headed toward the east block. Through the block door was a hallway leading to a window. Four doors faced the hall. Immediately to the right was a door with a large silver "1" on it. To the left was our door.

"Welcome home." Flynn smiled, placing his chip next to a pad to the right of our door. The door lock clicked, and he pushed it ajar.

"After you." He bowed slightly at the waist with his arm folded across his stomach.

Our room was simple but spacious. Straight ahead was a window. Along the left wall were two elevated beds, the kind with desks underneath. On the right, there stood two wardrobes on either side of a door.

"That is the bathroom we share with the guys in

room four. You're all right with sharing a bathroom with three men, right?"

Alarm shot through me. Before my brain could tell my mouth what to say, Flynn went on like he hadn't said anything unusual. "Would you like the window bed or the one closest to the door? I prefer the window myself, but I'm willing to negotiate."

"I am fine with the door side," I mumbled.

"Great!" Flynn grinned and climbed his bed. Lying on his stomach, he closed his eyes. "The valets should deliver our luggage sometime during dinner."

"How do you know all this?" I asked, feeling uninformed.

"I got here early to scope out the place," he replied with a voice that said he was up to something.

I didn't respond, but sat in my desk chair and began giving myself a mental pep talk. *You can do this, Kai. It seems difficult now, but you will manage. Your task is worthy. The rules are unreasonable. Oh man, this is too much. I will never pull it off. No, stop it! You are just as clever as any boy. Look at it this way: your lack of feminine curves will finally come in handy. Yes, it's possible. I know it. I just have to access the right information.* Pumped up, I smiled.

That's when I realized Flynn was staring at me. He made no attempt to hide it. Finally, he asked, "Tell me why a girl, such as you, would come to an all-boys university?"

Before fear could get a grip, I started to laugh. I just couldn't help it. I was hysterical. Sides aching, I wiped tears from my eyes. "Did you just ask me, 'What's a girl like you doing in a place like this?'"

Flynn's serious expression flew from his face, and he hopped down from his bed. "I guess I did, but if you want pick-up lines, I can do better."

Seeing his grin sobered me. I buried my face in my hands. "Oh man! I am so screwed."

"I can do that too. I do appreciate a good scheme, though. Let me in on it, and I won't turn you in," he conspired in a whisper.

I sighed, both relieved and anxious. "First let me say, if you try anything while I am sleeping, you will be sorry you ever looked upon my face."

He grinned but held up his hands in surrender. "Mysterious...and noted."

"Okay," I began. "You know how magic surrounds us and pulling it from the atmosphere is how everyone utilizes it?"

He nodded at the common knowledge.

"Air, water, and earth elementals are trained to manipulate the elements around them to accomplish various ends. But fire elementals can create fire. I am convinced that other elementals could create their elements too, not just manipulate what is already present. I came here to figure out how to do it." I looked up nervously.

He considered what I said, then replied, "That's the craziest theory I have ever heard. I love it. And what's more, I will help if you share your findings with me."

"You will help me keep my identity safe and

research this accepted impossibility?" I said, unconvinced.

"I get to cause many loud diversions and slap accepted principles in the face; what's not to love?"

I analyzed his expression for signs of deceit. After taking in his earnest face, I figured he would at least keep my secret for a while.

"What do we do first?" he asked.

I hesitated. My plan didn't have concrete steps.

"I guess we have to check out literature on how fire elementals create fire?" I said, uncertain.

"Sounds good. By the way, what is your *real* name?"

"Kai."

"Well Ki-Ki, it is an honor to meet the first female to ever infiltrate Capital University. I couldn't have done it better myself." He bowed again at the waist, then looked up, eyes sparkling with undoubted mischief to come.

The afternoon waned into evening as Flynn gave me tips on how to better pass as a man. Flynn and I went to the dining room on the lookout for Leif and Reid. The dining room had a large window in the back with a buffet table stretched in front of it.

Four rows of four round tables were arranged between the entrance and the buffet table. Each table had eight chairs. Some of them were occupied and some were empty. *Maybe some of the students haven't arrived yet.*

We found Reid and Leif at a table on the far-left side of the room. Flynn did his full-arm wave to his brother to tell him to save us seats. We headed to the buffet table to grab some food. Plates fully loaded, we walked to the table where they waited with six empty seats.

Leif was practically bouncing in his seat when we arrived. "Kie! Guess what? Reid and I are roommates. He is so nice. He let me have the window bed." He smiled so widely I thought his cheeks must hurt.

"That's great, Leif. I am rooming with Flynn," I said, sitting next to Leif.

Flynn sat beside Reid, who was on Leif's other side. Reid nodded to his brother. They began some type of silent communication outsiders could never truly understand. It looked to me like Flynn was saying something was afoot. Reid asked a question. Then Flynn's eyes flicked to me. Reid's steady gaze settled on me.

It wasn't cold as I expected it would be. It was quiet and curious. *Well, I guess it was too much to think Flynn could keep my secret from his twin.*

Meanwhile, Leif was telling me all about the plants that grow in their dorm room. "There is ivy all along the walls and this flowerpot in the windowsill, and Reid said we could plant whatever we want. Did you get a flower box?"

"No, but we don't practice the magic that makes plants grow," I replied.

"That's true," Leif said, looking sad that we didn't have flowerpots, too.

I shoveled down a few bites. Patti told me that while men can have nice table manners, they are not required the same way they are for women.

A loud clapping drew everyone's attention to the window side of the room, and the talking quieted.

Dorm Leader stood, demanding attention. "Eat hearty," he said. "Early tomorrow, we meet outside by the front door. Disciplined magic use requires a strong body and a powerful will. Every student, including the scholar and military students, will be participating. We will walk from our front lawn to Training Field together. Your physical training begins then and will continue every morning until you graduate. Sleep well. See you at first light."

CHAPTER 2

From somewhere unknown and decidedly evil came the sound of a loud gong. The intercom blared this sleep-shattering sound to tell all students to get up and get ready. Five thirty in the morning brought the raw sensation to my ears. I clenched my eyelids tight and curled into the fetal position under my covers.

Cold air suddenly slammed my skin. "Come on, Ki-Ki!" Flynn yanked the blankets off my bed.

I groaned and cursed.

Flynn's eyes widened with mock surprise.

"Is that any way for a lady to talk?" he asked.

"A lady wouldn't have to get up so early," I shot back.

"Regretting your decision to forego the privileges of the weaker sex?" he prodded.

That had me up and throwing my pillow at him.

I raced him to the bathroom and won. Locking the door to our room behind me, I also made sure to lock the door to room four. I definitely wiped the seat before I sat down. All I needed was to sit in I-don't-want-to-know-what to make the morning gross. Quickly finishing, I flushed, washed my hands, and went back to our room.

"Do you think you can change into your exercise clothes before I finish?" Flynn teased, making it sound like a challenge.

"I bet I take less time to get ready than you, Miss Priss," I taunted.

"Challenge accepted," he said, closing the bathroom door.

Crap! I rushed to my wardrobe and grabbed my exercise uniform. There were a few combinations allowed by the school. When manipulating the cloth to copy the uniforms I saw in the catalog sent to Patti's older brother, Dane, I chose to mimic the running pants and jacket as they would best cover what little figure I had.

Cloth manipulation is considered a staple lesson for girl-children. How could we make suitable wives and mothers without this skill? I was never very fond of it, so I often neglected to practice. I don't think I could have managed without Patti's help.

"Pulling magic to place natural fibers in an attractive pattern is an art, Kai," Patti always told me. *"They must be woven and shaped. They have to fit the wearer and make him or her look more attractive."*

Though I was so sick of hearing that speech, I was glad Patti was good at cloth manipulation. Otherwise, I would have been in trouble though it didn't stop her from refusing to do the class uniform. She thought I needed to feel the "joy and wonder."

At least she fixed my attempt, making it was passable.

Flynn exited the bathroom with his hand over his eyes. "Will I be scarred for life?" he asked, peeking through his fingers.

"Beat you," I said, tying my shoes.

He pouted his lips and whimpered.

I rolled my eyes.

"Hmm, that usually works. I will find your weakness and exploit it! Bwa-ha-ha," he said with a mock villain laugh.

I laughed in return because it sounded so ridiculous. "Meet you down there," I said, headed for the door.

"Fear not, Ki-Ki. I shall rendezvous with you at the appointed time and place!"

It took little time to walk out the block door, down the stairs, and out the front door.

It was not yet six o'clock, so the daylight simulator had not been activated. Twelve hours of what we were told was sun-like light, from six to six. Twelve hours of complete darkness, well other than what was lit by fire or, if you were wealthy, blue shard-powered lights, which of course our prestigious university had.

I couldn't wait to start classes. As a girl-child, I did not get to learn more than the very basics. *This device simulates daylight. This is how long daylight lasts. You don't need to know how it works, just how it will affect your ball or dinner party.*

Looking up at the blackness above me made me think of all the tutors I had as a child. They were so frustrated by my curiosity, many of them quit. *Why do we live underground? When did we get here? Are we all that are left, or are there others?* I had so many questions and so many quiet-time punishments. It didn't get better when I went to Social School, either.

I bet those tutors and teachers never saw this coming. Today, I start taking real classes with real professors. After physical training and breakfast, all first-years had to attend an orientation. Then the learning would begin. I had Introduction to Magical Theory and History 101: Beginning of Subterranean Habitation, which were both required courses for first years. Following lunch, I had Air Elemental I. Those classes were three days a week. On the in-between days, I had Developing Peace of Mind and Magical Devices, also required for first years.

This line of thought led me right to Sei. *Thank you, Sei, for giving me this opportunity. I will write to you soon.*

I wonder what my parents would say if they knew I was coming here rather than that fancy finishing school to which they had sent me, I thought, stretching to loosen my limbs for the sure-to-be grueling exercise. The thought made me shudder. The glowing started from somewhere far above, pulling me from my thoughts.

I wasn't kidding when I said ladies aren't up early. It is considered indecent. Therefore, I had seen the morning glow only a few times in my life. Every time was breathtaking.

It started with a soft warm glow, like the ember that promises a cheerful dance of flames. It would grow in brightness slowly but steadily over the next hour so as not to shock the eyes. At five in the evening, it would start to dim and turn off at six.

Though the dimming is also beautiful, it always held a note of fear and uncertainty for me. I preferred the glowing much more.

I must have been engrossed to not notice a warm body so close to me. The look of awe on my face while watching the glowing had him downright staring at me.

I ducked my head and lowered my eyes. Then, remembering what Patti had told me about men and dominance, I squared my shoulders, faced him, and stared him down. He was the second-year who had given me my room chip. He had dark hair and dark eyes. As I stared back, his expression went from unreadable to bored. He looked away first.

Did I win?

A long arm snaked around my shoulders. "Who's your friend, Ki-Ki?" Flynn asked louder than necessary. The second-year walked away. Flynn watched him carefully.

"Let's go," Flynn said, dropping the arm around my shoulders and tugging my arm. I followed him through the crowd to where Leif and Reid waited. Reid was stretching, and Leif sat on the ground looking pale.

"What's wrong, Leif?" I asked, crouching beside him.

"Oh. Hey, Kie," he said flatly.

"Did you sleep all right?" I asked.

"Yeah," he replied.

Guessing his change in mood had something to do with the physical training ahead, I said, "Just stick with me. I am sure they will go easy on us the first day."

He looked at me with a flicker of hope.

"Everyone here?" called Dorm Leader. "We're headed out. Follow me."

I gave Leif a hand up. Dorm Leader started toward Training Field at a jog. We all followed the path around the dorm and through the trees. Eventually, Training Field appeared ahead. Heading into the nearest arch, we entered into a large grassy field surrounded by nine arches, which were connected at the tops. At the far end was a shooting range.

Students from Military Dorm were already lined up on the grass. Their uniforms were red while ours were blue. The rest of my dorm mates and I filed into rows next to them. From one of the eastern gates came the scholar students wearing yellow. They lined up with us. We all faced a very big, serious-looking man in red.

"Good morning," his voice boomed at us. "I am your physical training instructor, Master Graham. We will begin this semester by gauging your physical abilities. Dorm leaders, lead your charges in a run."

After running around the outside of the arches more than a few times, we were told to line up again. Master Graham walked along the rows of students memorizing the faces of new students and our various degrees of fatigue. Some students were collapsed where they were supposed to be standing. Some were not even breathing heavy.

I was aching, sweating, and out of breath, but I managed to stay on my feet. Leif was on the ground. Reid and Flynn were breathing hard but not as much as I.

I was skimming the rows looking for the dark-haired, dark-eyed second-year to see how he was faring when Master Graham stepped in front of me. He towered over me, scanning my face and posture. Taking it all in, he asked my name. He nodded acknowledgement when I answered and moved on to Leif.

I watched carefully, protective instincts ready to spring. Master Graham's face took in Leif's sprawling form. His features softened slightly. "It will be difficult at first, but you will get there," he encouraged.

Leif looked up at him. Like me, he had feared the worst. Several emotions passed quickly over his face: uncertainty, relief, and then determination. Leif struggled to his feet and said, "Leif" in a clear voice. Master Graham nodded and moved on.

After reviewing the ranks, Master Graham released us for breakfast. "Work hard. Get stronger. See you tomorrow," he told us.

Breaking formation, Leif, Reid, Flynn, and I grouped together as we hobbled toward our dorm. On the way, we compared schedules. I had Intro to Magical Theory with Leif, History 101 with Reid, and Air Elemental I with Flynn.

Reaching the dorm, we split up to shower and change. Once in our block, Flynn and I met the residents of room four. Mal was broad-shouldered with chestnut hair. Eyrie was leaner with sandy hair and pool eyes.

We hammered out a shower schedule: me, Eyrie, Flynn, and then Mal. Flynn argued I should go first because I smelled the worst. I think he was just being considerate of the level of hygiene I was used to.

I left them in the hallway smelling each other to determine who really smelled the worst.

I approached my wardrobe to grab my uniform. Above the bar where my uniforms hung was a shelf where I kept my shower supplies. Next to the supplies, sat a small oak box. Inside the box was my most precious possession. Thinking about it resting in there safely melted away all the fatigue from my physical training.

I grabbed my class uniform from the wardrobe. It consisted of black trousers, a white button-down shirt, a black blazer trimmed in white, and a blue tie with white stripes, which announced my elemental first-year status. The tie and stripe colors depended on what school and year a student was. Elemental students had blue ties with white stripes for first years, green stripes for second years, pink stripes for third and purple stripes for fourth. The stripe colors were the same for all students. The base color for scholar students was yellow. For military students, it was red.

After grabbing my uniform and supplies, I locked myself in the bathroom. Stepping under the hot water, I felt it ease my tight muscles. One of the best perks of pretending to be a boy is having short hair: less fuss and less shampoo. Shower complete, I toweled the water from my skin and used unscented moisturizer. *Hey, boys can have soft, healthy skin too.*

After binding my chest and dressing, I rubbed the towel over my black hair, avoiding my eyes in the mirror as I had always found my sapphire-blue eyes unsettling. They were far too bright and looked especially big when my hair was wet. I brushed and artfully tousled my hair, then brushed my teeth and headed out.

Telling Flynn I would meet him at breakfast, I went to the dining room.

The dining room was much more crowded than the previous night. I filled my plate with hearty breakfast foods: eggs, meats, and breads. Walking a straight line to the table we sat at before, it was too late to veer when I realized the dark-haired, dark-eyed second-year sat there alone. I sat directly opposite him at the large table for eight to discourage conversation. He seemed mildly surprised anyone sat there at all. I kept my head down and ate quietly.

A student with a blue and pink tie sauntered to the table. "Hey Ryn, I see you've finally got yourself a girlfriend," the third-year said, putting his hand on the table and leaning over the second-year.

Alarmed at being discovered, I looked up at Ryn to see his reaction. He kept eating, pretending as though the lean third-year was just an insect to be waved away. *Oh, I guess he said girlfriend to be mean, not because he knows I'm a girl.* I sighed at myself. *Again with the paranoia?*

The third-year turned in my direction, having

not elicited a reaction from Ryn. He sized me up with a quick once-over with his eyes. He must have determined I was an easy target because he sauntered my way and took the seat beside me.

"You keeping Ryn warm at night, Fresher?" he stage-whispered at me.

A gravy-soaked, floppy slice of meat smacked him on the side of his face. It slid slowly down, landing in a limp, wet heap in his lap. Time halted. Talk at the tables around us stopped. Heads swiveled our way.

Ryn calmly ate, unconcerned, with a space on his plate where meat used to be. I stared at Ryn, stunned. Gravy-face recovered after a few drawn-out seconds.

He turned to Ryn, rage in his eyes, and stood slowly. The meat in his lap splooshed to the floor.

I held my breath for his reaction.

Ryn appeared to be calmly chewing, but his muscles tensed ever so slightly, ready for action.

"Excuse me," Flynn said politely tapping the lean third-year on the shoulder. "You are in my seat. Also, you have something on your face." Flynn's serious expression split into his natural grin as he pointed the lean third-year's attention behind him where Dorm Leader stood.

"Do we have a problem, Des?" Dorm Leader asked the lean third-year.

"Of course not, Dorm Leader," Des managed through clenched teeth. He left with a look at Ryn that told everyone this wasn't over.

Dorm Leader looked at the rest of us sternly for

good measure, then walked away to police someone else.

Flynn sighed with satisfaction and plopped down next to me. "You were almost collateral damage, Ki-Ki. Lucky you've got me around," he said, mussing my hair.

"Thanks, Flynn," I said with relief. "And thank you," I said a little louder at Ryn across the table.

He looked surprised but bobbed his head in acceptance.

Reid joined us. While Flynn filled him in on all the excitement, Leif sat down on my other side. Reid appeared thoughtful and concerned after the recitation. His reactions surprised me again as before.

I am glad I have History 101 with Reid. Being around him without Flynn and Leif will give me a chance to figure him out. I snickered to myself. *I want to get a read on Reid. He seemed cold and distant at first, but his face is so easy to decipher. And it expresses unexpected emotions.* A tug on my sleeve pulled me out of my thoughts.

"Orientation," Leif said, and all the first years shuffled toward Student Hall.

CHAPTER 3

Leaving Elemental Dorm via the front door, we walked along the path to Student Hall.

We passed four lecture halls on the right. Closest to Elemental Dorm was Air Hall then Earth Hall followed by Fire Hall. Water Hall was the closest to Student Hall.

Shuffling through the lobby of Student Hall, we entered a large auditorium capable of seating the entire student body, just short of 400 students.

The elemental students filed into seats behind the scholar students, already assembled in the front rows. I sat between Flynn and Leif with Reid on Flynn's other side. Excited murmuring emanated from the assembled students. The military students arrived a few minutes later and filed in behind us.

A short, older man approached a podium on the stage.

"Welcome new students to Capital University," he began.

"Congratulations on your acceptance. I am Dean

Cobb, alumni of the Scholar School. I hope your time here will be full of learning as well as the start of life-long friendships. However, do not forget that you are here to study. Only ninety-eight students are accepted every year, thirty-two for each school and eight for each major. Do not make us regret our decision to select you. Whether you were admitted because you passed the rigorous entrance exam, a prestigious master referred you, or you come from an illustrious family, any one of you can fail. We will not sully the alumni that came before you by graduating poor performers. Observe that the three classes above you no longer have ninety-eight students."

He paused for effect, then continued, "Because the graduates of this university benefit all of Terrenus, we receive most of our funding from the public. We are also funded by private donations. Therefore, most of your supplies are provided. Do not let the people of Terrenus down. Work hard and stay focused. Then, at graduation, you will have earned your purple tie and gold pin."

He left the stage as we applauded. A student with a yellow and purple tie stood and told us to proceed to the bookstore down the hall to receive our bookchips and supplies. We followed him there like a good herd.

The bookstore was already packed with upperclassmen getting their course-bookchips. Aisles of drawer-filled shelves lined the store. Each drawer contained bookchips with a label on the front naming its contents. Locating the appropriate drawers was simple. Navigating through the crowd was a different matter altogether.

After conquering the crush, we headed to the front counter. The man behind the counter was handing out RWDs, reading-writing devices—flat screens with slots on the sides for bookchips—and pen-like devices to write with. We grabbed a handful of blank chips to write on from the bin next to the counter.

We were also given brown leather bracelets. Each one featured a square of wood that touched the wrist when worn. We were instructed to put them on directly and never to remove them. We stuffed our supplies into messenger bags from a pile next to the exit. Leif and I parted from Flynn and Reid to go to our first class: Introduction to Magical Theory.

Student Hall had many classrooms on the upper floors. Leif and I took the stairs to the second floor. We found the assigned classroom and took seats at one of the tables occupied by two military first-years. I sat next to a muscular redhead. The students talked softly while waiting for the master.

"This will be a great refresher," Leif said to me.

"You know a lot about this subject?" I asked.

"I always excelled at theory. It is practical application that gives me trouble," he replied.

"I know only basic theory. I would really appreciate some help studying," I said.

"I would be happy to help you, Kie." Excitement lit his face. "If you don't mind having me as a partner," he added quickly.

"I think you will be a great help," I smiled reassuringly. *Maybe tutoring me will give Leif more confidence.*

A squat man wearing spectacles entered at the front of the room and faced the assembled students.

I turned on my RWD and inserted a blank chip, preparing to take notes.

"This is Introduction to Magical Theory. I hope you are all in the right place. I am Master Hart." He was interrupted when a disheveled scholar student burst into the room.

Everyone turned toward the student, who blushed crimson and rushed to the first available seat.

A few blinks later, Master Hart continued, "This course is the foundation of all future theory and practice courses. It requires a lot of reading and memorization. Fair warning."

Master Hart then went over what would be expected of us in order to pass the course and progress to the next course in the series.

"Let's jump in, shall we? Magic surrounds us on all sides. We breathe, eat, and drink it; it permeates our beings. Anyone can pull it from the air for many purposes. It can be pulled to manipulate the elements, create art, power magical devices, or do everyday housework. For more difficult tasks, like expanding Terrenus, pulling and controlling the flow requires a disciplined mind and body. This is why you are here and your sisters are not."

Chuckles escaped from some of the students.

He continued, "We have found the female mind is not peaceful or disciplined enough to waste resources training them to use advanced magic. Their bodies are not capable of reaching the strength and endurance necessary to control the flow."

The redhead next to me snorted softly.

"However, girl-children do learn basic household magic, such as cleaning and cloth manipulation. This has the added benefit of freeing you from wasting energy on mundane pursuits so you may progress to more advanced magic. You are all here to learn such magic so you can become scholars, elementals, or fill the military ranks."

I went from indignant to amused. *Who says women can't learn and handle advanced magic? Where was that study published? They just want someone else to do the housework. What would Hart say if he knew I was a girl? I would love to see an argument between Sei and him.* I peeked at Leif; he was wearing a dark frown. *What's wrong with him?*

Master Hart continued to explain how our bodies pull, process, and release magic. "Simple magic does not require any awareness of the level of magic present. The user simply knows it is present and imagines the result. For instance, you have a bolt of cloth and imagine how you want it to look. More advanced forms of this magic require the user to be aware of and gauge the magic's frequency. This is the type of magic learned by scholar and military students. Elemental magic is performed by synchronizing like with like. This is a complex process that will be covered in individual elemental courses. Your assignment for the next class is to read the first chapter of your course-bookchips on the prerequisites for pulling magic. Some of these I have covered, but your text goes into more detail. Write and submit which of these prerequisites you feel you have and how you propose to attain the others. Class dismissed."

Released, I turned to Leif. "What's going on, Leif?"

"I've only ever heard speeches like that from my father," he replied, upset.

"What about your theory tutors?" I asked.

"My tutor taught me to love magic. He always said, 'with love and determination, anyone can succeed at anything.' I never felt like he was excluding women." An uncertain look crept onto his face.

My heart warmed. *Leif is such a gentle and kind man.* Arranging my features in a serious smile, I said, "I agree with your tutor. Don't let Hart's opinions sway what you have always felt to be true."

Noting the muscular redhead next to me listening in, I turned to him, a challenge written all over. He grinned in response.

"I would have loved to see my sister's response to that little speech. I am not ashamed to say she kicks my butt on a regular basis," he laughed. "Roan," he said, holding out his hand.

We introduced ourselves and shook hands.

"Where are you headed?" he asked as we exited the classroom.

"History 101," I said.

"Magical Devices," Leif said.

"I'm headed to Magical Devices myself. Mind if I walk with you?" Roan asked Leif.

Leif was surprised but pleased, and accepted the offer.

I waved goodbye to them, telling Leif I would see him at lunch. Then I headed toward History 101, on the lookout for Reid.

CHAPTER 4

Leaving Student Hall, I turned right. The first building on the right was History Hall. I found Reid already seated in the assigned classroom. I took the seat next to him at the end of the table. He nodded at me when I made eye contact.

"What did you have first?" I asked him when it was clear I had to start the conversation.

"I had Magical Devices," he replied.

He really is not going to offer additional information.

"How was it?" I asked eventually.

"I believe it went well," he responded.

Okay...awkward.

His expression was not cold but guarded. Floundering, I tried to decide how a guy would break the tension with another guy. Then I remembered Flynn had already told Reid I was a girl, so I could act normally. Just this once, I blessed Flynn's loud mouth.

Dropping the façade, I relaxed my features to

show my concern and turned to Reid. After all, he had shown me concern.

"Are you all right?" I asked.

"Why did you get my brother involved in this?" he said, losing his temper.

Taken aback, I must have looked hurt because his anger quickly fizzled out.

"I didn't involve him. He just knew, and he volunteered to help," I explained.

Reid sighed heavily, "Of course, he did."

He sat quietly thinking for a while. The classroom started to fill with students.

Diplomatically, he turned to me. "Fine. Count me in." He held out his hand.

I shook it uncertainly. He mustered a small smile, and I smiled back. *Will Reid let me in now?*

A throat-clearing quieted conversations and directed everyone's attention to the front of the room. A handsome man wearing a white, collared shirt and a purple tie under a black sweater leaned the backs of his legs against the master's desk.

"Welcome to History 101: Beginning of Subterranean Habitation. Thank you all for coming. I am Master Wilhelm. You will be joining me this semester on a journey through history," he smiled seductively.

He personally gave each of us a bookchip. After inserting it into our RWDs, we went over the syllabus together.

"Who knows why we left the surface?" Master Wilhelm asked.

He called on a military student in the front row. "Because of the Ice Age," the student answered.

"Very good," Master Wilhelm rewarded him with a smile. "Let's start there."

"Year 1 marks the beginning of the Subterranean Era, or SE. In 1 SE, a group of around 500 people, led by Paul Greene, took refuge from the dropping temperatures in a large underground cave. Greene and his team of scientists theorized the closer they got to the core, the better their chances of survival. And so it was that Terrenus was eventually founded, and here we are, safe from the frozen wasteland that is the surface, in 453 SE. The journey from the beginning until now is what we will be covering during your time here at Capital University. The account of the beginning was recorded in the journal of Sharma Greene, Paul Greene's wife and fellow scientist. Your assignment for our next class is to read the excerpt from Sharma Greene's journal in your course-bookchips. Write your thoughts, impressions, and questions about what she writes. Class dismissed."

Collecting our supplies, Reid and I strolled toward Elemental Dorm for lunch. While passing Water Hall, he turned to me as though he had decided something.

"May I tell you something? I feel it will help you better understand me and my brother."

"Of course," I said, eager for information.

He looked around and saw students all around us. Grabbing my hand, he dragged me off the path.

We went around Water Hall and stood amongst the trees surrounding Peace Garden.

He faced me, staring into my eyes intently. Realizing he still held my hand, I wiggled my fingers, and he dropped it quickly. I waited patiently for him to collect and order his thoughts.

"I am sorry I was so cold and angry with you before. I keep everyone, other than Flynn, at a distance. That is what surprised me, in fact. Flynn usually does the same. I was shocked he took to you so quickly. It made me question how you elicited such a reaction. I thought maybe you threatened him or me. I apologize for suspecting you. We have closed ourselves off since Ayana." His voice gave way to emotion.

I stepped closer to him and placed my hand on his upper arm. He stared into my eyes, searching. *What is he looking for?*

"Ayana was our cousin though she was more like a sister. She was bright and happy. She spread her joy to everyone around her. Her parents died tragically when we were all very young, and we took Ayana in. Mother doted on her, trying to give her as much love as she could muster so she would feel at home. Mother hired the best tutors to teach Ayana anything she wanted to learn. No one suspected her art tutor was anything other than honorable. He told us he was taking her on a trip to Capital Art Museum, and they would be back in a few days. He never came back. Ayana's body was found violated and battered on the side of the road. My parents contacted Police and Patrol, but he was never found.

Our family hasn't recovered," he finished woodenly, not daring to feel the emotions.

Tears streamed down my face. I wrapped my arms around his torso with my head over his heart. Though he returned my embrace, I do not know whether it was meant to comfort him or me.

I don't know how long we stayed like that. Eventually, I stopped crying and became aware of just how close we were. I loosened my grip around him and eased a little space between us. He released me and looked down, embarrassed and confused. I wanted to reassure him, so I placed my hand on his upper arm again and smiled softly.

There is no need to be embarrassed. I don't feel embarrassed for comforting a friend. I pulled away because we can't stand here embracing in the woods all day.

"Thank you for sharing that with me, Reid," I said, willing him to be at ease. He nodded and straightened his uniform, which was wrinkled where I had clung to him.

Tell me I didn't snot on him, too! A dark spot over his heart told me only tears had seeped into his jacket. No slime, no snot. *Well, that is something, I guess.*

"Shall we go to lunch?" he asked after clearing his throat.

I mustered all the lightheartedness I could, "Onward!"

We continued eastward through the trees until we hit the winding path that led to Peace Garden. Heading south, we turned left once it intersected with the main path. Passing Earth Hall and Air Hall, we arrived at Elemental Dorm while lunch was in full swing. Grabbing plates and food, we walked to our customary table.

Leif, Flynn, and Ryn sat at our usual table. Knowing Reid and Flynn would be having a silent conversation, I sat between Leif and Ryn. I acknowledged Ryn with a polite smile, then turned to Leif, who was gulping down enormous amounts of food.

"You're going to make yourself sick eating that much," I said.

He swallowed with effort. "I asked Roan how he got so big. He said he eats a lot."

I smiled as he went back to eating. Settling into my own food, I reviewed my day so far. A pointed throat-clearing drew my attention to Ryn.

"How do you like your classes so far?" he asked tentatively.

Hearing his hesitation, I tried to sound friendly and conversational. "I liked history and Master Wilhelm. I don't think I like Master Hart, and I don't know much about theory. But Leif said he is good at it and will help me study." *He looks so uncomfortable. Why did he talk to me?*

"You can ask me if you get stuck," he grumbled.

"What was that?" I asked. *I heard him, but I don't want his help if he's unsure.*

He cleared his throat, and a bored expression slid into place. "I did well in that class. If you really can't figure it out, I can lend my expertise."

I smiled internally at his change in attitude. "I

don't know. Leif seems pretty confident. He will be a great tutor."

His boredom shifted to disappointment.

"Still, you've already taken the class. If Leif and I need help, may we ask you?" I asked, not wanting to torment him longer. Smugness warred with boredom. I had to look away so I didn't laugh.

Long fingers gripped my shoulders, and a face appeared close to mine over my left shoulder. A slight turn of my head revealed Des, way too close to me. "Aren't we snuggly," he whispered, breath hot in my ear.

I tried to shrug him off, but he held tight. His face blocked Ryn's from my view. A look to my right showed three pissed off first-years. All three stood slowly; Reid was the one to speak. "You are going to remove your hands," he growled.

"Why would I do that?" Des asked sweetly.

A pitcher of water from the center of the table hovered over to us and slowly poured itself over Des' head. He shrieked and shoved it away. Flynn laughed uproariously, identifying himself as the culprit. Des turned his fury on Flynn, who ran from the room. Des followed in hot pursuit.

Relief chased away my fear, and I let my bunched muscles relax. Flynn's prank left me soaked. "I better go change," I said to no one in particular and went to my room.

After my squelching walk upstairs, I was grateful to get out of my wet uniform. Pulling on dry pants, I heard a gasp behind me. The opened door revealed Leif standing wide-eyed and mouth agape.

"Close the door!" I yelled, clutching my shirt to my bound chest.

"S-s-sorry!" Leif squeaked and slammed the door.

Crap! I will be lucky to last a week the way things are going. I finished dressing and cracked the door. Leif sat on the floor, knees bent to his chest.

"Leif?" I asked gently.

"Yes?" he responded through the hands covering his face.

"Please come in," I said, opening the door for him. He peeked through his fingers and crept in. I closed the door behind him. He looked terrified, ready to bolt any second. I slowly walked to my desk and sat in my chair. He relaxed slightly once he had a clear path to the door.

"Leif..." I started.

"I'm sorry, Kie! The door wasn't shut all the way, and I came to see if you were all right. I didn't know!"

I nodded gravely in acknowledgement. "What are you going to do, Leif?" I asked softly.

He looked confused, then resolved. Clearing his throat, he said, "Of course, I will be honorable. If you and your parents agree, I will fulfill my duty for having shamed you, but do you think they will marry you to someone so young?"

I burst out laughing. I realized Leif was totally serious, which made me laugh harder. Gasping, I said, "No, Leif. Are you going to tell anyone at the university I am a woman?"

His expression cleared into comprehension. "But you must be here for a good reason. Of course, wanting to learn is a good enough reason," he mused.

"I am here for a very good reason, Leif," I said. "I want to ensure no one will suffer the way Toby did."

After a long pause, I continued quietly. "I told you before I am from the rim?"

He nodded.

"The rim is very different from Capital. We are close to the walls. Of course, that is where the expansion happens. As Capital grows and other towns get larger, the elementals at the rim have to dig outward," I said in a soft tone. Taking a deep breath, I continued in a whisper.

Leif moved closer to hear.

"Toby was my younger brother. Sweet and sensitive, he followed me everywhere." A painful lump began to form in my throat, and my eyes blurred with tears.

Leif timidly moved to kneel before me and took my hand. His uncertainty was replaced with comforting resolve as he processed my expression. He forced his clear blue eyes on me, so I could focus only on them holding me. Reassured, the lump eased a little.

"I was always fascinated by elementals, so I used to sneak out to the dig sites and watch them. We had an expansion zone that was shut down as unviable."

Looking only at Leif, I persevered, taking strength from his clear, steady gaze and his thumb gently stroking the back of my hand.

` "One day, Toby and I went exploring the unoccupied tunnels dug by the elementals to test the viability of a zone. A cave-in cut off our air. We weren't strong enough to move the rocks. We cried for help for a while and then huddled together, hoping someone would come for us. We were trapped in there for a few hours. They found me unconscious." I took a shuddering breath, but my voice grew stronger as I was enveloped in Leif's unanticipated presence.

"After I woke, I asked after Toby. No one would answer. They would just cry and turn away. Finally, when I was well enough to get out of bed, I found Toby in the parlor. He was laid out, surrounded by candles." Perhaps anticipating an emotional outburst, Leif covered my hand with his free hand. While comforting, the gesture was unnecessary. He had already soothed me.

"I screamed and cried and rushed out of the house. Near our house is a large group of trees with a spring in the center. Toby loved that spring." I cheered a little, thinking of better times.

"I ran there and cried until there were no tears left. A kind old man from my village, an air elemental, comforted me and returned me home to my parents. I visited him every day after that, and he eventually explained that Toby had suffocated. I asked him to teach me air magic, and he did. Later, I learned that had I known air magic when Toby and I were buried it would not have made a difference. The old man told me fire is the only element that can be created. Air can just be moved, and there was no vent in that tunnel. I still don't understand why air can't be created, too. I asked him, but he didn't know. He agreed it may be possible if you apply fire magic principles to air magic. But he didn't know fire magic, and there weren't any fire masters near us that would teach a girl. So we hatched a plan: he would get me into Capital University, and I would research how to create air."

Leif knelt quietly, processing the information I had piled on him.

"Who is this old man?"

"I call him Sei."

A stunned look slapped Leif's face. "Sei? Master Sei, the accomplished air master who dropped out of society for a quiet life?"

"He must be accomplished for his recommendation to get me into Capital University," I shrugged.

"Wow! You studied with Master Sei?" His eyes gleamed.

"Leif, will you help me?" I gripped both his hands in mine, pleading.

"But what can I do?"

"Help me figure it out, and keep my secret. I only have basic knowledge of magic, and I am not very disciplined. You've had more education, especially in theory."

"Do I have to keep it a secret from Reid and Flynn?"

"They already know," I replied, hoping he wouldn't be angry. Unfazed, he squeezed my hands.

"You can count on me." He smiled.

"Thank you, Leif." I hugged him.

Not knowing how much time had passed, I said,

"Maybe we should make sure Flynn is all right. Des looked like murder."

Leif agreed, and we hurried down to the first floor. Flynn lounged on a couch in the common area. The wideness of his grin was comparable to Reid's frown. Seeing us, Reid smoothed his frown to a more neutral, welcoming expression. We stood closely so only they could hear.

"I see you are in one piece," I said to Flynn.

"What can I say? I am light on my feet." He floated to a standing position.

"Well, Leif knows. He found me trying to get dry," I told them. Reid turned his stony disapproval on Leif.

"You sneaky, sneaky man," Flynn tsked.

Leif lit up bright red.

"All right, boys," I said, trying to preemptively calm them down. "What say we meet after class, do our homework, and get in some research on my query?"

"Good idea. Let's meet at the main library at three?" Reid suggested. We all agreed.

Flynn and I said our see-you-laters and headed toward Air Hall for Air Elemental I.

CHAPTER 5

*E*xiting Elemental Dorm, Flynn and I entered the first hall on the right, Air Hall. We found our classroom and took two seats. Because Air Elemental I is the introductory class on air magic, the only students in the class are the eight air elemental first years.

"You must be pretty excited, Ki-Ki," Flynn grinned. "You finally get to openly throw air around."

"I am actually kind of nervous. I only know basic stuff. I am not even close to you with your floating water pitchers."

"Don't worry. You will catch up. They will start us off as if we don't know anything because the students have such varied backgrounds," he reassured, patting my shoulder.

After a few minutes, Mal and Eyrie entered and waved a greeting. Four other students, who I had seen around our block, eventually trickled in. Finally, a shaggy blond man in comfy clothes flopped into the classroom. Rather than occupying the instructor's desk, he took a student desk in the front row, straddling the chair to face the class.

"Hey there, new air elemental students," he slurred. "I am the instructor for this course. Just call me Johnny."

We all stared, speechless. Johnny seemed to enjoy our bemusement.

"I know you all come from different back-grounds, so we will take it slow while I evaluate your individual needs."

I glanced at Flynn. He grinned and waggled his eyebrows.

"On days we don't have discussion, we will have lab. Starting tomorrow, we will meet at Air Field at 2:30." He paused to make sure we understood that we would be meeting for his class every day.

"Okay. So the very basics of air magic: You measure the available magic, match like with like, then visualize the desired outcome. The more prac-ticed you are, the more quickly you can execute these three steps. Your peace of mind classes will also help you learn to measure the magic. For air magic, you match your breathing to the available magic's frequency. Practice is the best way to distin-guish frequency and match it. Later in the semester, discussion classes will be replaced with labs. Ques-tions?" He looked at each of us in turn. No one had any questions.

"Sweet. See you tomorrow then." We watched him flop from the room.

"Wow, that was short. *And* no homework?" I commented.

Flynn nodded with satisfaction. "I like it."

"We don't have to meet Leif and Reid for a while. What do you want to do until then?" I asked him.

Whatever he had in mind, it looked like trouble. "Follow me," he said hypnotically.

We left Air Hall and took a right. Passing all of the elemental halls and Student Hall, we were on the scholar side of campus. We passed History Hall and the Science and Engineering Building, and turned right into the Art Building. The first floor of the Art Building had an art supplies store, much like the campus bookstore. Flynn grabbed supplies like he knew exactly what he was looking for. He got clay and a tube of blue paint.

We left the art supplies store and turned left, taking the path between the Art Building and the Science and Engineering Building. I followed him, mesmerized by the look on his face. It was a combination of mischief and wickedness with a dash of mirth and a sprinkle of determination.

We walked around the library and through the trees until we hit the path connecting Scholar Dorm and Training Field. We crossed the path and stopped in the group of trees surrounding the instructor offices.

"This is your first lesson in the practical application of air magic, so pay attention, Ki-Ki." He grabbed the clay and started molding it into a ball. "How much do you know about making pottery?" Flynn asked.

"Almost nothing."

"Okay, from the beginning then. When preparing to make pottery, potters wedge the clay to get all the air bubbles out as they can cause problems later. Think of wedging like kneading dough. We are going to use those air bubbles to create a pocket in the clay ball."

He picked up a thin stick from the ground and stabbed the clay ball, then removed it.

"I am going to use the airway I just created to make an air pocket in the middle of the clay."

He closed his eyes and regulated his breathing. The clay ball began to swell. Then he grabbed the tube of paint and squirted it into the stick-created airway.

"When filling the air pocket with paint, make sure you don't fill it completely. There has to be air left in the pocket, too." His concentration was replaced by that wicked grin. He held the clay ball aloft in reverence.

"Complete." He nodded with satisfaction.

I followed as he crept toward the instructor offices. We hid behind the trees facing the entrance. Flynn held his hand up, and the clay ball floated out of it to hover above the door.

A number of students and masters entered and exited with no activity from the ball. It hovered in anticipation. Eventually, a familiar squat, spectacled master exited the offices. The clay ball bobbed menacingly. It expanded, then splattered clay and blue paint all over the stunned Master Hart.

Flynn didn't wait for a reaction. He grabbed my

hand and made a break for the library. Reaching the entrance, he slowed his pace and entered calmly, dropping my hand to open the door. We took the stairs to the fourth floor. Approaching an open table in the group study area, he began emptying both our bags to show how we had been doing homework the entire time.

After setting the scene, Flynn put two chairs side-by-side and sat me into one, then took the other. He pulled his chair close and leaned his head in. To onlookers, we seemed to be studying collaboratively.

"We made it," he whispered. "So what did you learn from our lesson?"

"That you are a maniac."

"Now Ki-Ki," Flynn said primly. "I am sure he gave the same ridiculous speech in your class as he did in ours. The man needs retribution, not to mention a sense of humor. I am generous enough to provide both until he lightens up."

"I know he is a jerk, and he probably deserved it, but you shouldn't have. What if we get caught?"

"I will think of something."

"That reminds me. Why did you break that window on our first day?"

He answered as an instructor. "Practice is how we get better. Do you think I can splatter clay balls on the first try? Of course not. It took a lot of practice with air pressure. That mishap in Reid's room was one such failed experiment, but I stamp this latest foray a success."

I sighed, "You are incorrigible."

He grinned. "You love me."

I rolled my eyes. "Let's just get to work."

I was just finishing my Magical Theory assignment when Reid and Leif found us.

"You will never believe what we heard!" Leif whispered too loudly. "Hart was attacked. Apparently, he was hit with a paint bomb."

I arranged my features to appear shocked. "Really? Was he hurt?"

"No, just enraged. They are having difficulty discovering who did it."

Flynn remained silent and expressionless. Reid narrowed his eyes at his twin. "You didn't," Reid accused.

"I have no idea what you are referring to, dear brother," Flynn preened.

Reid half growled, half sighed, and sat down across from me.

Leif watched their exchange and grinned at Flynn. "You are the master."

Flynn grinned back.

I think Flynn is becoming a bad influence. Leaving Flynn and Leif to their grin fest, I turned my attention to Reid. Making eye contact, I gave him a weak smile. "I don't think we will get caught," I soothed.

"*We...*" His eyes flashed in Flynn's direction.

"She wasn't in danger. I will take full responsibility if we get caught," Flynn promised.

"Wait a second..." I protested.

"Don't worry about it, Ki-Ki," Flynn interrupted.

Reid's temper began to wane and a sinful grin danced on his lips, "I wish I could have seen it."

Wearing that grin, it was the first time Reid and Flynn truly looked like identical twins.

Not you too, Reid. Don't encourage him. "If you are all finished congratulating Flynn, we should finish our homework," I censured. They all looked chastised, so I added, "The sooner we finish the more fun we can have."

We shared a smile and dove into work. Inserting my history text chip into my RWD, I navigated to the excerpt from Sharma Greene's journal.

Living below ground seems more plausible than we had hoped. The diggers found plant life while excavating today. We are encouraged that the seeds we brought with us may be able to survive.

We welcomed a new baby into the group. Violet Algren birthed a boy, Charles. This happy news is accompanied with the death of old Tucker Smyth. Tucker lived a full life and did not let age hinder his participation in our venture. We hope little Charles will have a full life as well and never have to experience the cold as we have.

Everyone is adjusting to the change in pressure though the youngest are having the easiest time.

Ellie brought me more 'treasure' today. She is such a little scavenger, always returning with little stones or shells. This time she brought me a crystal shard. It is a pretty transparent blue. At her insistence, I made it into a pendant by wrapping it in wire. I strung it on a cord for her. I don't think she will ever take it off.

We finally entered the cavern the diggers have been trying to get into. The tree limb blocking the way was removed. Inside the cavern was the most bizarre chamber. The roots of a large tree surround the walls and ceiling. Peppering the cavern is a strange black metal. We have yet to determine its properties.

Ellie collapsed. She was found at the entrance of the cavern. The crystal around her neck was glowing faintly. I removed the crystal. She is at home recovering.

We hypothesize the crystal interacts somehow with the contents of the cavern. Parameters for experiments are being discussed.

We have discovered that the black metal interacts with the crystal by creating an energy field. Unfortunately, we discovered too late that the tree engulfing the cavern is also important to this interaction.

The tree acts as an insulator. Anyone touching the crystal or metal when they touch each other will be killed unless he or she also has skin contact with the wood of the tree.

My assistant Reggie discovered this at the cost

of his life. Proximity appears to also be a problem, which is why Ellie collapsed but recovered. All further experiments will be conducted while in contact with the tree's wood.

AFTER READING about Reggie's fate, I was grateful for the leather bracelet with the piece of wood that clung to my wrist. Writing my thoughts and impressions, I completed my history assignment.

Reid and Leif were still reading, and Flynn was writing his history response. I told them I was going to start researching and to catch up with me when they were finished.

I went in search of the nearest catalog station. The station looked like a large RWD; the bookchip was the library catalog. I searched the catalog for introductory bookchips on fire magic and found a few that looked promising. Writing down the bookchip numbers, I went to the second floor, where I could find the bookchips associated with those numbers.

The shelf I was looking for was in the far-right corner. Like the campus bookstore, the shelves contained drawers. Each drawer had numbered envelopes, and each envelope had the designated bookchip. Finding the appropriate shelves and drawers, I started to flip through the numbered envelopes.

Warm, humid breath tickled my ear. I spun around and found Des crowding me.

I glared at him, "What do you want, Des?"

"What is it about you?" he asked, ignoring my question.

"Why won't you leave me alone?"

He continued to ignore my questions. "Why is an air user in the fire magic section? What are you looking for?" He moved closer.

I stood my ground, defiantly facing him head-on. "I *am* here to learn. Is it a crime to read books unrelated to your major?"

He smirked. "I can see why my brother is intrigued with you. You are quite curious."

That downright confounded me. "Your brother?"

"My half-brother actually. We share a whore of a mother." Noting the color of his dark hair and the shape of his eyes and mouth, he did kind of look like…"Ryn."

"Oh bravo, you are very smart," he mocked. "But why is it that you, of all people, have made him waver? Since he started here, we have had a sort of agreement. I do what I want, and he doesn't stop me. The other students shun him, and he pretends not to care. This was our game, our beautiful dance. Keeping his head down is what allows him to return to my father's house and stay at this university."

I hadn't realized I was backing away from him until my back touched the shelf. He extended his arm over my shoulder and leaned in, blocking my exit.

"I will ask you again: what is it about you? Why will he risk my anger to protect you? Will you feel guilty if his actions make it so he has no home?" He leaned closer. His face was inches from mine.

I refused to withdraw and stared back into his dark blue eyes.

"Though, maybe I should thank you. Messing with him is so much more fun now," he whispered.

"Kie." A firm voice demanded my attention to the left.

Turning my head, I was surprised to see Leif over Des' extended arm.

"Excuse me," he addressed Des. "We have work to do." Leif grabbed my wrist and tugged gently.

I ducked under Des' arm and followed his lead.

Des seemed unperturbed. "See you around." He smirked, following me with his dark blue gaze.

Leif led me to a quiet study room, combing over me with his eyes. "Are you all right?"

I nodded, not trusting my voice. Satisfied, he began to shake and took long deep breaths.

"I have never done anything so dangerous." he mumbled.

"You did great, Leif. Thank you for coming to get me."

He turned to face me, and his expression darkened with displeasure. Shock confused me. *Leif is... angry?*

"You need to be more careful. How did you get into that kind of situation? What if he had hurt you? What if he had discovered you are a girl? You should avoid him or learn to defend yourself or both." Being censured by Leif was so much worse than anyone else.

"I'm sorry. You're right. I will learn to defend myself." My repentant tone satisfied him.

"I am sorry I was angry with you. I was just scared and worried. I am quite surprised at my own reaction." He laughed uneasily. "I guess I have never had someone need me before."

"Thank you, Leif."

Though Leif was still the weakest of the group, his drive to protect me seemed to be making him grow stronger.

"All right then," he pronounced. "Let's go back together and get those bookchips."

CHAPTER 6

We retrieved the bookchips without incident and returned to where Flynn and Reid waited.

"What happened?" they asked together.

"Nothing. We just had trouble finding the right drawers," Leif lied smoothly.

Reid and Flynn seemed unsure, but accepted his word because we had all assumed that Leif couldn't lie.

We each took one of the four bookchips I had found. I began skimming through *Creating Fire* by Walter York.

After a while, Reid said, "I think I found something." He began to read aloud from *Rekindling Humanity's Connection with Fire* by Jack Lily.

"Elemental magic works by matching like with like. For air magic, the elemental matches his breathing. For water magic, he regulates his heartbeat and thus the flow of his blood. For earth magic, he flexes and loosens his muscles. But for fire magic, the elemental must use his inner spark. He must match his soul's frequency to the frequency of the magic. This takes much more discipline and self-awareness, which is why fire elementals are the fewest in number."

We stared at Reid in silence.

"I guess the next step will be to find a fire elemental willing to teach matching soul frequency to an air elemental student," Flynn said.

We all made sounds of agreement.

We gathered our RWDs and bookchips to return to Elemental Dorm. I put the fire magic bookchips back in their envelopes.

"I will meet you outside. I am just going to take these to the front desk to be shelved."

Leif hesitated, reluctant to leave me alone. I smiled reassuringly and nodded to tell him I would be all right.

He went with Reid and Flynn as they walked on ahead of me. I waited to be helped at the front desk. The student in front of me was huge. Broad shoulders stretched his uniform as he hunched his blond head to talk to the person at the front desk.

As he left, he peeked over his shoulder, self-conscious that he was making others wait. I stepped up and handed over the bookchips for shelving. Turning to leave, I ran smack into his broad chest. He steadied me by grabbing my shoulders. A yellow and green tie stared at me before I raised my eyes.

My shock was mirrored in the face of this huge, second-year scholar student. Before he could say anything, I beckoned him to follow me. We left from a side door so we wouldn't run into Flynn, Leif, and Reid. I led him into a group of trees.

"Kai, what are you doing here? Why? Why are you dressed like that? You cut your beautiful hair!" Dane, Patti's older brother, lamented.

I didn't respond. I just let him calm down. When the shock wore off, I addressed him. "Dane, I am convinced it is possible, and I'm here to figure out how to make it happen. I will leave when I can make air."

His voice turned soothing. "We have talked about this. It is not possible. I know you are doing this for Toby, but you can't be here."

"You know my reasons. I can't leave." This is a fight we have had many times before. It was not going to be different this time.

"Master Sei got you in, didn't he?"

I didn't respond. That was answer enough.

He sighed, running his hands through his hair. "You are supposed to be at finishing school with Patti."

I snorted.

"I am sending you home," he resolved.

I stood my ground. "I'm not going."

He grabbed my arm and flung me over his shoulder. "You're in Elemental Dorm? We are going to get your stuff." He started walking, and I was reduced to begging.

"Please, Dane," I sobbed. "This is my one chance. I will go home or to finishing school as soon as I figure this out."

He stopped walking. "What if it isn't possible?"

"Give me two years. If I haven't figured it out, I will leave."

"One semester."

"Two semesters," I bargained.

He set me on my feet and stared skeptically. "Fine," he grumbled. "But when your time is up, you will go to finishing school."

"Thank you!" I hugged him.

He tilted my head up to wipe my tears. "You always get your way with me."

"Because you're the best." I smiled up at him.

"Oh my, are we interrupting?" Flynn asked suggestively. Dane spun his back to Flynn, Reid, and Leif, hiding me from view.

"They're my friends," I said into his chest.

"But do they *know?*" he whispered.

"Mmm-hmm," I nodded.

He eased his grip and turned toward them, keeping his hand on my shoulder. Leif's, Flynn's, and Reid's eyes all flickered to his hand.

"Who's your friend, *Ki-Ki?*" Flynn forced nonchalance but emphasized his name for me.

Maybe Dane won't notice. I looked up at Dane. His eyes turned flinty. *He noticed.*

"This is my best friend's older brother," I explained.

"Oh-ho, so not friends at all then," Flynn prodded.

Dane's expression furrowed in doubt. "Kai, I have known you most of your life," he said quietly, crestfallen.

"I'm sorry, Dane. I just always think of Patti first.

Of course, we're friends. This is Reid, Leif, and Flynn, my roommate."

Reid nodded, Leif smiled, and Flynn twinkled his fingers and grinned.

Dane growled, "Deal's off. You can't room with a man."

"That's enough, Dane. You told me you would give me two semesters. We agreed. Flynn is harmless."

"I think I'm offended." Flynn mimed an arrow to the heart.

"Besides." I turned an icy gaze on Flynn. "He knows what will happen if he doesn't behave."

"I already surrendered!" Flynn protested.

"Whatever retribution she has promised, mine will be much worse," Dane threatened.

"Likewise," seconded Reid and Leif.

Flynn sniffled. "Does everyone believe me a cad?" He looked around.

No one objected.

He sidled over to Leif. "Now, Leif. I don't want to hear that from you after what your peepers have peeped."

"What...?" Dane started.

"Dane, I know you do not want me here, so I can't ask for your help. However, can I ask that you keep my secret?"

"Kai," he said, hurt. "It isn't that I don't want you here. It's that you should not be here. I will not tell anyone, but I will say again: it's a waste of time. I don't think I *can* help, but I will always help you, Kai, whenever you need me. I wish you would have asked me before you made this jump." He gestured to my male attire.

"Oh, that's right," Flynn grinned. "You've seen Ki-Ki as a girl. So, Dane, tell us. How is she?"

Dane sputtered, and Reid smacked the back of Flynn's head, which didn't knock the grin off his face.

"Well." I gently removed myself from Dane's arm. "We had better head to dinner."

Leaving Dane to his business, the four of us started toward Elemental Dorm.

"So, Ki-Ki," Flynn said, putting his arm around my shoulders. "Was that your beau from home?"

"Not at all," I replied, pushing his arm off. "We are just childhood friends."

"Silly, Ki-Ki. You know not of men's hearts."

They were all silent. I looked at them each in turn. *What is* that *expression?* I gave up on deciphering them. "We should scope out the fire elementals at dinner to see if we can find someone to teach me."

"Yes, we should begin our search as soon as possible," Reid agreed. "It appears as though you don't have much time."

"Yeah," I murmured, thinking of my two-semester deadline. We slowed the pace and finished the walk in thoughtful silence.

Reaching the dorm, we split to drop our bags in our rooms. Flynn and I walked into the dining room together. Getting our plates, we sat with Reid, Leif, and Ryn, who were already eating.

Ryn's eye contact made me recall my close

encounter with Des earlier. I blushed and looked away. Though Ryn's deep brown eyes were completely different than Des's dark blue eyes, the similarity in shape was enough to make me remember the feel of Des's body heat as he leaned close to me. Ryn seemed confused by my reaction, embarrassed even.

"What is your major, Ryn?" I asked.

Seeing what I was after, everyone at the table listened for the answer.

"Water," Ryn answered, uncertain as to why I would ask.

"Oh," I said, disappointed.

"Why?"

"I just had questions about fire magic and thought you might know."

"Ask me anything." Des's soft voice startled me.

I felt my face get hot. *Where does he come from all the time?* "No, thank you," I said flatly. Ignoring him, I turned to Ryn again. "Could you recommend someone to me?"

Ryn seemed to enjoy me snubbing his brother in favor of him.

"Dorm Leader is probably the most knowledge-able. He is certainly the most accomplished, but he's very busy. Why not ask Ichii?"

This suggestion, along with my verbal slap, infu-riated Des. The candles on the table flared menac-ingly. Two drops from the water pitcher extinguished them with a hiss. Ryn and Des stared each other down.

"Thank you for your suggestion, Ryn. Could you point Ichii out to me?"

Making Ryn look away first gave Des the small victory he needed to retreat without shame. As he left, he traced his fingertips across the back of my neck, making an unfamiliar jolt shoot down my spine.

All the men at the table noticed this little intimacy but let it pass as Des was already leaving. Still, Reid's mouth flattened into a line, Flynn stabbed meat with his fork, and Leif grumbled into his food.

Ryn distracted me by pointing to a petite fourth-year at a table across the room. "That's Ichii. He is skilled and helpful."

"Great. Thank you." I smiled at Ryn.

His expression was stunned for a second, then confused. He bobbed his head in acknowledgment and began to eat quickly.

"What do you guys think?" I asked, gesturing toward Ichii.

"Worth a try," Flynn said.

Leif and Reid agreed.

After dinner, the four of us waited in the first-floor common area. When Ichii left the dining room and headed for the stairs, we caught his attention. He seemed surprised but amiable.

"I have some questions about fire magic and was told you are very knowledgeable," I explained.

"Go for it. I will help if I can," he encouraged. His approachable demeanor and bright presence made me trust him.

"I want to try an experiment, but it is secret. Will you help me but keep it to yourself?"

"It isn't illegal, is it?"

"No."

He stared at me intently. I don't know if he was judging my character, or reading my aura, or what. But after a minute, he smiled a bright beaming smile that said all was right in the world. "I will help you any way I can."

I thanked him, relieved, and told him my theory. He was surprised but thoughtful. I agreed to meet him in the second-floor meeting room the next day after a quick lunch. Then we said goodnight and went to our respective rooms.

After changing into our pajamas and climbing into bed, I heard Flynn get out of his bunk. A light brush of my hair had me flipping over to stare at Flynn next to my bed. His brown eyes peeked at me over the side.

"Ki-Ki?" he asked softly.

"What is it, Flynn?" I said, trying to sooth the vulnerability in his voice.

"I don't want you to leave," he whispered.

I reached out from under my blanket and put my hand on his head. The waves of his brown hair were soft, and the ends curled around my fingers. "I don't want to leave either, but I promised Dane."

He sneered.

"Oh, come on. We can still be friends. I will write to you. And, if I go to that finishing school, I will even invite you to the parties. Then you can show all those fancy girls how awesome you are."

"It won't be the same."

"I know, but what can we do?"

"Kill Dane."

"Shut up and go to bed," I laughed, ruffling his hair.

He placed my hand on his cheek, then withdrew to his own bunk.

I listened to Flynn's slow breathing and thought about how attached I had become in such a short time. *I am going to miss them, but Dane is right. I can't waste my time if my quest isn't possible. I'm glad I have a time limit.* Tears seeped into my pillow as I fell asleep.

CHAPTER 7

The next morning was much like the one before. Get up, change, jog to Training Field. The physical training was more specialized. We were put into smaller groups based on ability. Each group was assigned a leader of a higher ability. Roan was my team leader. Reid and Flynn were in a more advanced group. Leif was in a group that needed more work. Leif's determination was a welcome sight.

Teams were all given exercises based on ability. My team ran, then did sit-ups. Roan was a good team lead. He knew when to gently encourage and when I needed a kick in the butt. After we were finished, he told each of us what we did well and what we should work on. Apparently, I needed to pace myself better.

We were tired but cheerful. I returned to the dorm, showered, and went to breakfast. I felt warm and shiny after a good workout and a shower. Leif was gorging on food as I sat between him and Ryn.

"Thank you for suggesting Ichii. I think he can help me," I said to Ryn.

He stared at me blank-faced but nodded.

"Are you all right?" I touched his shoulder, concerned.

"Fine," he stood abruptly, looking panicked. "I will see you later." He left his food half-eaten.

I turned to Leif who looked up at Ryn's sudden departure. Leif looked back at me slack-jawed. Shaking himself, he studiously returned to eating.

What the heck? I looked to Reid for answers. He watched me from the corners of his eyes with an indecipherable expression. Flynn moved to Ryn's place and leaned toward me.

"You may want to tone it down a bit, Ki-Ki."

"Tone what down?" I furrowed my brow at him.

"Rub some dirt in your sparkle, will you?"

"What?"

"You are looking too...glowy," he whispered.

I just stared at him.

He leaned in closer to whisper in my ear. "You look too female."

I looked down at myself. Nothing overtly female was hanging out. I looked back up at him for more details.

"It's your face, Ki-Ki."

"What can I do?" I asked desperately.

"I don't know. Don't smile so much. That makes it worse. And, cool down before you are around other people after physical training or a shower. Like I said, you are all sparkly glowy." He emphasized by twinkling his fingers.

I stood. "I will be back." I ran to my bathroom and applied a cool washcloth to my face. After making myself less "glowy," I returned to the first floor to meet Flynn, Reid, and Leif in the common area. Leif handed me a napkin-wrapped bundle filled with bread.

"You left without eating," he explained.

"Thanks, Leif."

I ate the bread quickly as we walked to Peace Garden for Developing Peace of Mind. We all had this class together, but I would be alone for Magical Devices. Well, not alone, but without Flynn, Reid, and Leif.

Past Air and Earth Halls, we turned right onto the winding path that led to Peace Garden. The garden was in a large clearing covered in soft green grass and surrounded by trees. A small brook on one side made a pleasant water sound, and a brazier full of bright flames blazed in the center. Stones encircled the clearing inside the tree line.

A wispy instructor was directing students to sit cross-legged in a circle around the brazier. The water elemental students were told to sit close to the brook, but the rest of the elemental students, as well as the military and scholar students, could sit anywhere in the circle. I sat between Leif and Reid.

"All right, everyone," the instructor called to us in a hushed tone. "I am Master Tem. Is everyone comfortable?" He smiled.

"Developing peace of mind is essential to advanced magic. When at peace, you can better gauge the frequency of available magic. Peace of mind is much more difficult than it seems. It takes both concentration and fluidity of thought."

Master Tem produced a metal bowl and what looked like a thick wooden drumstick from somewhere on his loosely-robed person.

"We will start with a frequency exercise involving sound. Close your eyes. When you hear the tone, listen carefully and try to match the pitch frequency with a hum. This will give you a feeling of harmony that is very similar to matching magic frequency."

He struck the metal bowl with the wooden stick. The ringing penetrated my ears. I hummed, matching my pitch to the sound. The vibration from my ears met the vibration in my lips and nose. Harmony. Oneness. Peace. The ringing faded, and I stopped humming.

"Very good!" Master Tem praised. "Did everyone get it? Did you notice how there was one solid pitch with a hint of other tones? Magic is like that, too. Let's try something else. Do you hear that brook? Lovely, isn't it? Concentrate on that sound. Feel the water like it is flowing through you. Cool and refreshing. Do you feel it? Do you feel the frequency, the vibration? Strong and firm, yet yielding and pliant. Don't do anything with it. Just be aware. Let it flow through you."

The water sang in my veins. I felt it flow through me, humming a sweet tone.

"This is the first step to making magic. For water users, you would match your heartbeat and blood-flow to that frequency you feel. Air users and earth users would do something similar. For fire users, military, and scholar magic, it is more complex as you have to feel the frequency in the atmosphere with fewer physical stimuli. But this is a good start. As homework, I would like you to spend at least two hours feeling the frequency of this brook or, if you are adventurous, you can try the air, rocks, or trees of this garden. Be at peace," he finished.

I sat with my eyes closed, enjoying the peace awhile.

"Kai," Reid whispered, lips brushing my ear.

"What?" I jumped.

"You are going to be late for your next class."

Looking around, I realized everyone else had already left. *Crap!* I grabbed my bag and started to run to the Science and Engineering Building. "Thanks for telling me," I called to him over my shoulder. As I ran, I realized that was the first time Reid had called me by my real name. *He is definitely Flynn's twin, messing with me like that. Maybe I should get him back.*

I settled next to Roan just as the instructor walked in.

"This is Magical Devices. I am Master Oliver. Let's get down to business. Magical devices make our lives easier, yes? So what magical devices have you already been exposed to here at school? Your room chips, bookchips, RWDs? These devices are powered by your personal magic power. But you do not have to activate it, you say? Yes, because a concentrator draws the power without your knowledge. Living, eating, sleeping, breathing, we all consume the magical energy around us. This concentrator pulls small amounts of magical energy from the user to execute the device's function. When your room chips come into contact with the pad outside your doors, they pull small amounts of energy from you to unlock the doors. Energy pistols, used by Police and Patrol as well as the rest of the military majors, are powered by the users' magical energy too. However, energy pistols pull more energy than your room chips and can be dangerous to users if the settings are too high or if the users are fatigued."

"So what about the daylight simulator and small light generators? Well, blue shards power them. Discovered by Ellie Greene, you will learn about this in your history class if you have not already. I will demonstrate. Are you all wearing your bracelets? Let me see them."

We all held up our wrists.

"Excellent. Always wear your bracelets when in proximity to or in contact with black metal and blue shards." Master Oliver uncovered a device, which had been shrouded on his desk. "Behold, a light generator!"

The light generator was a black metal bowl with wires connecting the side of the bowl to a light bulb. A wooden dome with a blue shard embedded in the top sat next to it.

"Blue shards pull magic from all sources including the atmosphere and us. This is not a problem if the energy is not being directed. However, the reaction between blue shards and black metal causes the shards to pull all the magical energy from an unprotected person or area in an attempt to recharge itself. Wood from the Protection Tree acts as an insulator and protects a person or area." He placed a blue shard into the bowl, then quickly placed the wood dome over it. The light bulb illuminated.

"The dome ensures the blue shard in the bowl does not pull too much magic from the atmosphere. However, the blue shard embedded in the dome pulls just enough magic to regulate the flow being pulled by the blue shard in the bowl. While using blue shards and black metal is the most convenient and efficient way to power magical devices, both are in limited supply. Therefore, we must regulate their use and attempt to come up with alternatives. That is much of what the science and engineering students do once they graduate. Also, blue shards can be exhausted. Their exhaust times vary depending on the size and how they are being used."

He removed the dome and snatched the blue shard from the bowl.

"Your homework is to research a magical device of your choice and describe how it works." He made a shooing gesture with his hands, dismissing the class. Leaving the Science and Engineering Building with Roan, we turned left toward History Hall.

"What is your major, Roan?" I asked as we passed History Hall.

"Military aid."

"You mentioned before that you sometimes spar with your sister?"

"Yeah, she is probably going stir-crazy at home without me." He smiled fondly.

"Do you think you could teach me?" I blurted.

We paused outside Student Hall where he would turn to head toward Military Dorm. He turned to me and sized me up.

"What happened?"

"Nothing in particular. Leif just suggested I learn self-defense. Maybe I could bring him along too. He seems interested in bulking up."

"You're on," he nodded his approval. We agreed to meet the following day at three at Training Field and went to our respective lunches.

CHAPTER 8

I rushed back to Elemental Dorm, ate as quickly as I could, and went to the second-floor meeting room to meet Ichii. The meeting room was big and open with one wall covered in mirrors like a dance studio. There was a closet on one side where Ichii was shoving tables and chairs to give us space to work. I helped him clear the room, then sat on the floor in front of him.

"So what do you know about fire magic?" Ichii asked.

"The elemental must match the atmospheric magic with his inner spark, his soul's frequency," I recited.

Ichii nodded. "That's the basic theory, yes. How are you at reading magical frequencies?"

I cast my eyes down, fidgeting. "I can get to the surrounding frequencies. I have rarely gotten perfect pitch."

"I see. Have you ever felt your soul's frequency?"

"I don't know. How would I know if I have?"

"Your inner spark is what connects you to all that is magical, such as the elements, nature, and other beings. Have you ever felt connected, in sync, with someone else? Just for a moment you felt in harmony with him or her?"

"Yes."

"At that moment, your souls' frequencies were the same. You have to become more aware of it before you can manipulate it to match the available magic. Fire elemental students do a series of meditations to teach us to gauge our souls' frequencies. We can start by going through those, but you also need to work on gauging magical frequency. I assume you will do that anyway for your regular classes."

I nodded. "Can I see a demonstration?"

"Sure," Ichii said, knowingly. I leaned forward, excited to see fire magic.

Ichii closed his eyes and went very still. He slowly moved his feet apart and squatted a little. He positioned his arms in a circle with his left arm cradling the bottom of an invisible ball and his right arm lining the top. He began to slowly shift his weight from one leg to the other, making smooth arches with his arms.

At some point, his fingertips began dragging flames, making it appear like he was drawing large circles with fire. It was entrancing. The flames spread like wings, leaping and dancing in smears of yellow, orange, and blue. Eventually, the flames dissipated. He slowly dropped his arms and brought his feet together. Opening his eyes, he smiled brightly. I stared at him in awe.

"Amazing!"

"When do you want to start the meditation exercises?" Ichii asked me.

"As soon as we can."

"Same time tomorrow, then?"

I agreed.

He left, but I still had time before lab. I decided to go to the library and do homework while I could. My weekly schedule was filling up fast. Finding a table on the fourth floor of the library, I decided to write my Magical Devices' report on cameras and picture stands. I had always been curious how they worked.

I read about how cameras etch light images onto negative chips and, when the chip is inserted into the picture stand, a realistic image is projected from the stand. *Being able to behold the images of loved ones captured during happy memories sooths the longing heart. I should ask Leif, Flynn, and Reid to get their pictures taken before I have to leave.*

That thought turned my mood bittersweet. I finished writing my report just as I needed to go to Air Field for lab. I collected my bag and went to meet Flynn. I took the path from the library to Training Field. Entering the nearest arch, I walked across Training Field. Passing the arch that led to the professor offices, I went through the next arch to Air Field. Air Field was a big grassy clearing surrounded by trees.

Johnny was already there, lying flat on his back with a large sack next to him. Flynn lounged beside him.

"Pull up some grass," Johnny said without opening his eyes. I sat and waited for the rest of the class. Once everyone arrived, Johnny floated upright like he was rising from the dead.

"All right guys, let's see what you can do. We are going to gauge your levels. Partner up." We paired off into four groups of two and faced our partners.

"We are going to start with a gentle breeze. Try to ruffle your partner's hair."

Flynn went first. He stood with his feet shoulder-width apart and closed his eyes. After a few steady breaths, he extended his hand toward me. He opened his eyes and looked at me under heavy lids, puckering his lips ever so slightly. I felt a zephyr kiss my face and ruffle my bangs. Heat spread warmly from my abdomen, making me shiver. Flynn winked at me.

These men are going to be the death of me.

"Right on," Johnny congratulated. "Now, switch."

Nervous, I tried to calm myself. Planting my feet, I held my arms out slightly from my sides, spreading my fingers to feel the air. I closed my eyes and stilled my body. Concentrating on the air touching my skin, I could feel its familiar charge. The air was warm and heavy.

The frequency is low. Slow your breathing.

Narrowing in on the pitch, I breathed in slowly, matching my breath to the magic's frequency. A harmonic hum filled my body. I started the third step, visualization. Reaching my hand toward Flynn, I visualized the air around me moving toward him and ruffling his dark hair.

...lazy...

Dammit, Kai, pay attention!

I tried not to be distracted by the random emotion and continued my visualization. Opening my eyes, I kept visualizing. Flynn made eye contact and grinned. I imagined ruffling his hair as I had the night before when he had come to my bunk. His hair moved in a gentle breeze.

I did it!

Flynn's smile widened, and he nodded his congratulations.

"Excellent," Johnny praised. He approached the sack he had brought and dumped it. A variety of objects tumbled out, ranging in size and shape from paper confetti to rocks. The rest of the class consisted of us trying to float various objects. The final task was to float oneself. Flynn was the only one to pass them all. I was able to float the confetti and a handkerchief but nothing else.

I just feel so tired and...lazy...

Having a better idea of what our current abilities were, Johnny released us. "Catch you tomorrow." He waved over his sack-laden shoulder.

We walked through the arch to Training Field and exited the arch closest to Elemental Dorm. We talked and laughed with the other guys on the way back to the dorm.

The rest of the night and the next day flew by. Leif and I eagerly went to Training Field to have our first lesson with Roan.

"Self-defense has nothing to do with strength, bulk, or winning a fight. The goal in any confrontation is to incapacitate the assailant and/or get away safely. Because of your smaller statures, you have leverage and the element of surprise. I am going to show you a variety of scenarios and how to get out of them," Roan told Leif and me.

He called Leif to him and told him to attack in various ways. Then he demonstrated how to escape, evade, or counterattack each of Leif's attacks. He pointed out the body's weak spots and talked about incapacitating an opponent.

"There are many more scenarios, which we can practice next time. And then you can get some hands-on practice, too."

I started to get used to my new routine of classes, homework, and lessons with Roan and Ichii as the days started to slip away.

Eventually, I had to do laundry. I went late at night when no one else was likely to be there. There were various types of washing and drying machines in the laundry room. Some washing machines were for water users while nonwater users had to wash their clothes by hand. There were also drying machines for air users and fire users while others had to use the manual drying machines.

I was able to wash all of my clothes and load them into the air-drying machine without incident. The air-drying machine was like a closet with vents on both sides and a vat to catch the water at the bottom. The clothes are hung inside, and the air user pushes air through the vents to dry the clothes.

I opened the door to check how dry my clothes were. I still wasn't that great at creating a strong wind. *Maybe I should use the manual drying machine.* Just as I was unloading my wet clothes from the air-drying machine, Ryn walked into the laundry room.

Panic stuck in my throat as I stared in horror at the pair of women's underwear on the top of my pile of clothes. I snatched them and balled them into my fist.

"Oh, hey, Ryn. You are here pretty late."

His face flushed as he recognized me. "I always come here at this time."

I quickly loaded my clothes into the manual drying machine as he put his clothes in the water users' washing machine. I started to turn the crank that would dry my clothes, facing him as he began manipulating the water in the machine.

He stood, eyes closed, moving his arms in a fluid circular motion. The beauty of his movements captivated me. His body was strong and flexible like a river that could wear down layers of unmovable stone.

I didn't realize I had stopped cranking until he opened his eyes to unload the washer. His dark eyes found mine without error. They stared at me with an intensity that I didn't mentally comprehend, but my body reacted like it knew. My stomach dropped, and my limbs tensed. I looked away and used the tension in my body to crank the machine in earnest.

Peeking up at Ryn, I saw his shoulders were tense, and his jaw clenched as he brought his wet clothes to a dryer close to mine. I reached into the dryer and realized my clothes were finally dry. Walking a few steps to grab my basket, I didn't know the floor was wet by Ryn's dryer. As my feet slid out from under me, I prepared myself for impact.

Ryn quickly hooked my torso with his strong arm and clutched me to his chest.

I let out the breath I had been holding and looked up into his deep brown eyes, which were inches from mine. I opened my mouth to thank him, but my voice didn't come out. The intense look he had given me minutes before was nothing compared to the one he wore at that moment.

My whole body flushed. His intensity was soon smothered by embarrassment. Silently, he steadied me on my feet and went back to cranking the drying machine.

Hollowly, I retrieved my clothes and wished him goodnight.

Days blurred into weeks, and Ryn and I never discussed what had happened in the laundry room. I started doing laundry on a different day, so as not to repeat the encounter.

One day, after Air Elemental lab, Flynn and I walked back to the dorm with the rest of the first-year air students, laughing and joking as usual. Everyone was particularly high due the successful completion of midterms.

An attractive boy with blond hair flung his arms around Mal and Eyrie. "What are you up to this weekend, boys?" He laughed jovially.

"I have a date with my girl." Mal grinned as he punched the blond in the gut, making him laugh and drop his arms.

"Oh?" the blond prodded, punching Mal back. "What does she look like?"

"Don't worry about it," Mal replied.

"That doesn't sound good."

Mal grinned. "You just keep thinking that."

"How about you, Eyrie?"

Eyrie shrugged.

"What do you guys think of going to Jopin's?" the blond suggested.

"What's Jopin's?" I asked.

"Jopin's is a tea room and garden where all the finishing school girls go."

Maybe I can see Patti!

Seeing my excitement, Flynn said, "We're in."

The blond, who introduced himself as Marc, agreed to meet us in the common room after breakfast Saturday. We promised to ask Leif and Reid to join us. At the dorm, we all headed to dinner.

CHAPTER 9

Sitting down with Reid, Leif, and Ryn, we told them about our weekend plans. None of them seemed particularly excited. Ryn hesitated as though he was imposing.

"Won't you come with us, Ryn?" I asked, smiling at him.

He looked dumbstruck. "Oh, um...sure."

Flynn cleared his throat and raised his eyebrows at me. *Oh crap. The smiling thing. Right.* I forced a neutral expression. Ryn seemed to relax a little.

I finished dinner a little early so I could go to my room and write to Patti. I pulled out my RWD and put in a blank bookchip.

"Dearest Patti,

So much has happened in so little time! I want to tell you all about it. We are going to Jopin's on Saturday. Can you meet me there?

With love,

Kai"

I put the chip in an envelope and addressed it to Madame Bergot's Finishing School.

I took the envelope to the Student Hall mailroom rather than in the Elemental Dorm outgoing mailbox so it would reach Patti sooner.

Walking back from Student Hall, I took a detour via Peace Garden. No one was there.

I might as well do some Peace of Mind homework. I sat cross-legged on the lush grass. *I should practice with air since I am so far behind.* I removed my jacket and rolled up my sleeves to feel more air on my skin. Then I closed my eyes and concentrated.

...sweet...

Honing in on the frequency, I began narrowing in on the exact pitch.

...sweet...

I tried to force my mind away from the random emotion back to the frequency. I fought it for a while, but the feeling of sweetness kept breaking my concentration. I gave up and opened my eyes. The dimming was already underway.

A figure with dark hair sat by the brook with his back to me. *When did he get here?* I crept slowly around to see who it was. *Ryn.* I gazed at his meditating form, memorizing his features in detail while his eyes were closed.

His dark hair was straight and covered his forehead. The tips of his ears peeked out from the dark tresses. His gently-closed eyelids were hemmed in thick, dark lashes, and his cheeks and jaw begged for my fingertips to trace them. His slightly-parted lips intrigued me and beckoned my mind to an unknown place. I stared so hard that I flinched when his deep brown eyes opened. He flinched in return, not expecting to see me staring at him like a weirdo.

"Sorry," I said, offering no explanation for my shamelessness.

He cleared his throat and avoided eye contact.

Attempting to squash the tingle I was feeling, I drew attention elsewhere. "Des told me you are brothers."

"He called me his brother?" he asked, surprised.

"Yes."

"You should probably stay away from me," he whispered with downcast eyes.

"Why?"

"Because he will make your life miserable until you leave me alone."

I watched him carefully. "Do you want me to leave you alone?"

Meeting my gaze, his composure broke. "It doesn't matter what I want," he lamented.

"It does to me."

"I don't want to see anyone hurt because of me. This is my fault."

I crept closer. Close enough to reach out and touch him, but I didn't. "What is your fault, Ryn?"

"My brother's misery is my fault," he moaned.

I waited for him to continue.

"Our mother clearly prefers me over Des. Having entered into a loveless marriage with his father, she found love in an affair with my father. Outraged, her husband arranged for my father to disappear. She was so distraught that she left and attempted suicide, but then she discovered she was pregnant with me. Her condition for returning to his house, to avoid further scandal, was that I be allowed to live there. Des's father views Des and her as possessions. Never feeling a father's love and having a mother that openly prefers me, Des has been miserable most his life. If tormenting me is how he deals, I will endure it for my brother. But I cannot abide by him treating those around me harshly."

I sat in companionable silence, not trusting myself to keep my sex secret in my response. Finally, I put my hand on his shoulder. "You are not alone."

This pronouncement seemed to both shock and relieve him. He met my eyes with a look of gratitude. I removed my hand. A flicker of what looked like regret passed over his face. Then he looked startled and mentally slapped himself. The array of emotions passed so quickly that I almost missed them.

Seeming a little troubled, he stood. "It's past the dimming," he whispered. I looked around, surprised. It was dark except for the campus lights.

"Yeah, we should get back," I agreed.

We returned to Elemental Dorm in silence.

I entered my dark room as quietly as I could. Turning to shut the door, the light flickered on. Flynn sat, knees crossed and fingers laced, with a sharp expression in his eyes.

I jumped and clutched my heart, "Flynn, you scared me."

"Where were you?" he growled.

His seriousness censured me, and I hung my head.

"Doing Peace of Mind homework."

"Why were you gone so long?"

Indignant, I realized he had no right to question me. "What are you, my father?" I snapped.

"Your father isn't here to ask these questions. I can let him know what his daughter is out doing if you like."

I laughed bitterly, "Like he would even care."

That fizzled Flynn's anger. Concerned by my reaction, he approached uncertainly. "Ki-Ki, what do you mean?"

I clamped my mouth shut and shook my head. Flynn put both hands on my shoulders, "Ki-Ki..." I turned my head so as not to make eye contact. He gently placed his hand on my cheek and guided my head to face him, "Ki-Ki..." I cast my eyes down.

"Kai..." he whispered.

I looked at him, surprised. That was the first time he had said my name.

"What do you mean?" he asked gently.

I hunched my shoulders. "My parents don't really care what I do." I waited for him to protest, and he waited for me to continue. "Since Toby died, I have lived like a ghost. No one sees me or cares when I come or go. My parents were so devastated. It is as if we both died in that accident. I don't know if they blame me or what. I just know I don't matter." Tears, which I had been sure were long exhausted, escaped my eyes.

"I thought they sent you to finishing school?"

"Our housekeeper, Charlotte, takes care of everything. She knew they had planned to send me. She hired my tutors and enrolled me at the school. My father only had to sign the papers," I choked.

Flynn drew me tightly to his chest, his arms wrapping and encasing me. He let me cry until I was finished and shaking. His tight embrace held me together when I would have crumbled to pieces. Pulling back to look down at me, he wiped my stained cheeks with his thumbs.

"I am sure they do not blame you. You probably just remind them of all the happy times you all had together."

I sniffled.

He smiled at me warmly. "I will never understand how someone could think you are a boy. Why don't you splash cold water on your face and get into your pajamas? We can talk after." He ruffled my hair with his hand.

When I exited the bathroom, Flynn had a hot cup of cocoa waiting for me. Handing me the cup, he wrapped me in a blanket and sat me down on a desk chair. He sat on the floor, leaning back against my legs. I sipped my cocoa and absently stroked his dark hair away from his forehead. The ends curled around my fingers like soft rings.

"Won't the finishing school contact your family when you don't show?"

"Patti told them I wasn't coming. Like Capital University, it is publicly funded, so there isn't tuition to send back. They will just think I changed my mind."

He made a noise of acknowledgement. "Why did you choose Capital University and not a less conspicuous school?"

"Why did you?" I asked. "It's the best, I knew I would find the information I need here, and Sei is an alumnus, so he could easily get me in."

"Well, I'm glad you chose to come here," he whispered.

"Me too."

We sat silently for a while. I continued to sip cocoa and stroke his hair. He laid his head back, looking at me upside-down. His brown eyes, usually sparkling with mischief, were intense and serious.

"I can't imagine ever forgetting or ignoring you, Kai," he whispered.

My hand stilled on his hair as he held me with his eyes. I put the cocoa on my desk, feeling too warm to finish it. Licking my lips, I whispered, "Thank you, Flynn."

Tension built as our eyes remained locked. His gaze was strong and demanding. I bent my head toward him. No thoughts. No plan. No idea what I was doing. I sighed and my eyelids fluttered.

My legs and lap felt cold where Flynn's heat had been. I opened my eyes to see he had floated across the room. He wore a pained expression as he whispered, "Bathroom," and disappeared behind the door.

Breathing heavy and feeling a need I did not understand or know how to satisfy, I turned off the light and crawled into my bunk. The dreams I had did nothing to alleviate my desires. They did, however, give me insight into exactly what I wanted.

What do I do to get rid of this feeling? The throbbing was becoming almost painful. *Maybe a workout will help.*

I was dressed for physical training and out the door before Flynn was out of bed. Outside, I stretched before our morning exercise. My skin was overly sensitive, and the rub of my clothes was making everything worse. I tried breathing through the shivers, but every time I started to calm down, images from my dreams flooded my mind.

I jogged to Training Field, not waiting for Leif, Reid, and Flynn. I arrived pretty early. Only a few students were there warming up. I wanted to be worn out, to get rid of this excess energy. It worked. Physical training made my limbs ache and took all my thoughts away.

Success! I felt satisfied with myself and headed toward the dorms. Until I saw Leif, Reid, Ryn, and Flynn, long-limbed and waiting for me as I exited Training Field. My wicked dreams returned to the forefront of my mind along with the throbbing need.

CHAPTER 10

*L*eif waved at me happily. Reid smiled and nodded. Ryn looked uncomfortable but made eye contact. Uncharacteristically, Flynn did not grin and wave at me. He flinched, avoided eye contact, and turned his back to me. Hurt replaced the need as my stomach bottomed out.

Flynn, I'm sorry...

We walked back together. Leif chattered about I don't know what. Reid watched me closely, having noticed something was off. Ryn seemed to be at war between openly concerned and confused. Flynn walked with his own thoughts.

In our room, I quietly collected my clothes to shower. Flynn, who had been pacing the floor, stopped and faced me. I looked at him and waited for him to speak as he clearly had something to say. He opened his mouth, then clamped it shut.

Finally, he declared, "It didn't happen."

I stared at him.

"Can we pretend like last night didn't happen?"

"Nothing *did* happen." I spoke the truth but felt crestfallen.

He sighed, relieved. "Good." His grin back in place, he said, "You better hurry. I'm starving. I didn't get a lot of sleep last night."

Well, at least he is acting normal again.

I showered and went to breakfast. Flynn joined us shortly after. Everyone at the table seemed to relax when they saw Flynn back to normal. I tried to bask in the return of his fun-loving self, but it was bittersweet.

The day wore on, and I began to agree that maybe Flynn was right. *Nothing happened. Not really. For all I know, nothing happened to him at all. I was tired and upset. He comforted me. He is a great friend. I don't know what that feeling was, but it was probably a fluke.*

I was completely convinced by the time Leif and I went to Training Field to meet Roan that afternoon. We had a great lesson. We graduated from self-defense and had moved on to sparring. By the end of the lesson, we were both sore from being thrown around.

"Are you feeling better?" Leif asked as we walked to Elemental Dorm. I looked at him surprised. "You seemed off earlier. It looked like you and Flynn had had a fight. I thought I would give you a chance to work it out before I asked."

I didn't even know Leif had noticed.

"We're fine," I assured him. "Nothing happened."

The rest of the week took forever. I was too excited about seeing Patti.

My regular classes were going all right. Leif helped me with Magical Theory, and he really was a great tutor. I was doing well in Roan's lessons, but not so much in Ichii's. The meditations that were supposed to help fire users feel their souls' frequencies were not working for me. I didn't know what my soul was supposed to feel like. I only felt a flurry of my emotions. And, when I tried to gauge magical frequency, I kept getting distracted by random emotions that weren't mine. This was a problem I had always struggled with when doing magic. Sometimes, I could block it out. Other times, it broke my concentration. Ichii seemed unperturbed. He encouraged me by saying it would be more unusual if I excelled right away.

Finally, it was Saturday. We still had to do physical training in the morning, but the rest of the day belonged to us. I didn't have many clothes other than my school uniforms, so I wore a plain black suit with a green tie. Flynn and I met Leif, Reid, Ryn, Eyrie, and Marc in the first-floor common area after breakfast. Everyone looked so handsome, hoping to attract the young women at Jopin's.

A spark of jealousy chased that thought. *They are all going to meet girls. I am a girl, too...But there is no time for that now. I am here to figure out a fix for Toby's problem. Still...*

We exited the large gates across from Student Hall and entered the streets of Capital City. The walkways were crowded with people, and blue shard-powered buggies and animal-drawn carriages clogged the streets.

It seemed everyone was out and about. It was so busy that our group got separated more than a few times. Fighting our way through the crowds, we arrived at the trolley station. Climbing aboard, we rode though the bustling city until we reached our destination.

Jopin's was in a quiet neighborhood, close enough to the city center to attract patrons yet far enough to provide a peacefully tranquil atmosphere. Jopin's primarily catered to young ladies and gentlemen looking to make acquaintances in a chaperoned, controlled environment.

It had a square, quaint façade with pink flowers under the windowsills. Upon entering, a host showed us to a drawing room where small groups of young men and women talked, sitting on uncomfortable-looking couches and sipping tea.

I scanned the room for Patti and found her near a window. The outside light sparkled on her golden curls. She was chatting and laughing with another girl. I broke from the group and walked straight to her. Noting my approach, she waved and called to me, "Why, Mr. Stephenson! How wonderful it is to see you again. Imagine seeing you here!"

"Ms. Nord, how do you do?" I bent over her hand. Her companion seemed surprised and intrigued by my presence. "And who is your charming companion?"

"This is my schoolmate, Ms. Shale. Ms. Shale, this is Mr. Stephenson. He lives close to us and is a friend of my brother." I greeted Ms. Shale as I had Patti.

"Mr. Stephenson, how is your dear mother faring?" Patti asked, concerned.

"I am afraid she is not well."

"How dreadful. Shall we take a stroll in the garden, and you can tell me all about it? Please excuse us, Eliza dear." She grabbed my elbow. We abandoned Ms. Shale to walk the garden in the back.

On the way out, I noted my party. Marc stared, dumbfounded I found a lady to engage so quickly. Eyrie browsed the bookshelf at the far end of the room. Flynn was telling some girls amusing stories. Reid tried to look interested as a girl talked about tea. Leif was positively surrounded by solicitous girls and looked uncomfortable while still managing to be a perfect gentleman.

Be brave, my friend. I will come back for you.

Ryn was sitting between two very pretty girls, having what looked like a pleasant conversation. He saw me leaving with Patti, and an odd expression crossed his face. It looked like jealousy. I looked at Patti on my arm, all sparkling curls and rosy cheeks.

No wonder. Patti is clearly the prettiest girl in the room. Sorry, Ryn. You can talk with her later.

Patti and I strolled casually along the stone paths of the beautiful garden until we reached a secluded bench. Sitting, she turned to me in eagerness.

"Tell me everything," she demanded without preamble.

She made the expected gasps and sighs in all the appropriate places. Here and there she would interject choice phrases, like "that idiot" when I told her about my encounter with her brother.

She was disappointed her tutoring was not flawless enough to fool Flynn, but she was pleased her help with my uniforms was a complete success. Finally, I relayed what had happened the night before with Flynn, or rather what didn't happen. She nodded sagely.

"So have you ever felt that way? How do you make it stop?" I asked after describing the hot, painful throbbing.

She stared at me with the most serious expression I had ever seen her wear. "You really don't know?" she asked skeptically.

"Well, I certainly can't act out my dreams."

"Of course not, you have to take care of it yourself." She raised her eyebrows significantly.

"How..."

"When you feel like that again, go to your room alone. Explore the feeling. You don't have to fight it," she whispered delicately.

"Maybe it won't come back."

She laughed. "Oh, it will come back."

That settled, she asked, "Who do you like best?"

"What do you mean? I like them all. They are great friends."

"Oh Kai, you are hopeless. Let's go inside and take a peek, shall we? Introduce me to them."

We returned to the drawing room. I steered her toward Leif first as he was in need of some help. He was being swarmed. He reached out to me like I was a lifeline.

"Kie, where did you go? Can I join you?" Then he noticed Patti, who was still sparkling. "Oh, excuse me, Miss." He bowed and looked at me expectantly.

"Ms. Nord, this is..." I stumbled. *I do not know Leif's last name!*

He saved me by saying, "Mr. Algren, but please call me Leif."

Patti and I stared at him flabbergasted. Neither of us spoke for so long it became rude.

Patti recovered first. "Leif, I am pleased to meet you. Thank you for taking such good care of my brother's dear friend. He can be a little absent-minded at times."

"Not at all, Ms. Nord. Kie has been a great friend to me."

Algren! That can't be right. Leif is a direct descendant of one of the founding families? Patti pinched my arm discreetly.

"Yeah, we even spar together," I blurted.

Patti looked scandalized. I had told her I was learning self-defense, but I hadn't said I was sparring as well.

"Do not fret, Ms. Nord. We do not hurt each other."

"Well, I suppose boys will be boys."

After chatting a while, the girls Leif had left were becoming impatient. He reluctantly agreed to take a turn around the garden. I declined his invitation since Patti wanted to meet the others. Even though it had been her idea, she looked disappointed. Leif also looked disappointed, then overwhelmed by female enthusiasm.

I scanned the room to see who the next target was. Flynn and Reid were the closest. We drifted toward them. As we approached the twins, they cut off their conversations.

"Ms. Nord, this is Mr. Flynn Williams and Mr. Reid Williams." Flynn and Reid stepped forward in synchronized motion. They each grabbed one of Patti's hands and bent over it. "Ms. Nord," they said in unison. Then they looked up and smiled dazzlingly at her.

I had never seen Patti look embarrassed until that moment. She flushed and whispered, "Mr. Williams."

I wasn't even the object of this attention, and I felt charmed. I narrowed my eyes at the pair. Flynn grinned his wicked grin. Reid looked at me nonchalantly. *Sometimes, I feel you are the more dangerous brother, Reid. They enjoy this. Don't relax, boys. I will get you back.*

Patti recovered when the girl Reid had been talking to started talking about tea again. Patti looked at me significantly as if saying, "I see what you mean."

We separated from Flynn and Reid to search for Ryn. He had moved to the window and was talking with Ms. Shale.

"Ms. Nord, this is Mr. Breshire. Mr. Breshire, Ms. Nord," I introduced them.

Ryn bent over Patti's hand stiffly. "Ms. Nord," he said coolly.

"Mr. Breshire." Patti tried to smile but faltered in the chilly atmosphere.

Ms. Shale pierced the silence that followed. "Mr. Stephenson, I do hope your mother will be well soon." I looked at her, confused.

"My mother is taking good care of her, Eliza," Patti saved. "We are neighbors," Patti explained to Ryn's puzzled expression.

He rearranged his features to look bored.

Ms. Shale continued to be solicitous about the details of my life. What do I study? Where did I grow up? Do I have any siblings? Do I like art? Music? What have I read?

The longer this went on, the more Ryn's mask of boredom slipped. Finally, he slammed his cup in his saucer. We all stared at him.

"I need more tea," he explained angrily and stomped from the room.

I asked the ladies to excuse me, promising to say goodbye before we left, and went after him. He plowed past Leif as he was returning from his garden walk. I pursued him outside. He walked quickly to a secluded part of the garden, unaware that I was following. Facing a corner where two garden walls met, he stood tensely, clenching his fists.

I grabbed his shoulder. "What was that about?" I demanded.

"Why did you follow me, Kie?"

"I was worried. What's wrong?"

"You should have stayed inside." He spun around and pinned my back to the wall. He towered over me, eyes closed and breathing hard.

"Ryn?" I whispered tentatively.

He opened his eyes and searched my face desperately.

I looked back, concerned.

"Kie..." he said in a husky voice.

Without thinking, I reached toward him to comfort the lost look in his eyes.

He grabbed my hand in his and held it to his chest. The lost look was gone. A decision had been made. His lips crushed mine urgently as his whole body pressed against mine. The throbbing returned with a vengeance as I clutched to his chest. But I wasn't fighting. I was giving him everything he gave me. His hands traveled from my face to my lower back to pull me even closer.

When his scorching lips left a trail along my jaw to my ear, I gasped. I was lost, drowning in the hot spring that pumped through my veins. Until he nibbled my ear and whispered, "Kie..."

Kie? Who's Kie?... I am a boy. Ryn thinks I am a boy. My desire curdled into the sickness of rejection. *He doesn't want me. I'm a girl. If he likes men, he will be disgusted when he finds out.* I pushed him away, and he looked startled. "We can't," I gasped. "We are both men." My excuse was lame since he knew how socially unacceptable it was before he'd kissed me. But, it was the only response I could think of that a man who had just willingly kissed another man would say.

"I know. I know!" he said miserably. "But I can't deny my feelings for you anymore. I am not interested in men. I have struggled for weeks, but I don't have the strength to fight myself any more."

What should I do? Should I just tell him that I'm a woman? I can't afford to tell anyone else, and he will not be good at hiding it if he likes me that much.

"I can't."

"I understand. It took me a while to come to terms with the idea. I have never been attracted to a man before, only you. Think about it. I will wait. I won't give up until you tell me there is no hope."

I was going to tell him to give up hope right then, but something in his earnest expression stopped me. I righted my disheveled appearance and said, "We should be leaving."

We returned to the drawing room as nonchalantly as possible. Reid and Flynn, who seemed to have been looking for me, noticed something was off immediately. Leif was too bombarded to notice his tea was cold let alone whatever expression I was wearing. Reid and Flynn excused themselves from their company.

"What happened?" Flynn asked under his breath.

"Nothing," I said quickly. "Can we leave?" I tried to appear tired, which didn't take much effort. Then I took my leave of Patti, promising to write. Ms. Shale seemed terribly disappointed at our departure. Marc and Eyrie decided to stay longer.

Flynn snatched Leif from the flurry of females, and Ryn trailed behind. He looked almost pleased. Maybe not pleased, more like finally comfortable. The five of us took the trolley back to the university. Leif dozed, exhausted. Flynn and Reid watched me anxiously, and Ryn hummed cheerfully to himself.

We arrived just after lunch. It was clear Flynn and Reid wanted to talk, but I didn't know what I was going to tell them. *I can't tell them what happened with Ryn. I need more time to think.*

Leif was going to his room for a nap. Going to my room alone sounded like a good idea. I followed suit, claiming to be tired as well. Flynn and Reid reluctantly let me go. As I walked away, Ryn followed me. Stepping a little closer than necessary, he looked down at me with that needful look. I stopped, taken aback by the force of the painful throb that flooded my body.

"Sweet dreams, Kie," he said, low and with emphasis.

"Yeah. Umm...th-thank you." My teeth practically chattered with the shakes that overtook me.

"See you later," he promised.

I nodded, clenching my teeth. I nearly ran to my room.

CHAPTER 11

Making sure the door was securely shut behind me, I began ripping off my clothes. My hands shook, and I could barely unbutton my shirt. After much effort, I managed to get undressed. Standing in my underwear and binding, I still felt too hot. I removed the binding and climbed into my bunk.

I was relieved to feel the cool air on my skin and the crisp sheets under my barely-clothed body, but my inner furnace still blazed. I tried to go to sleep, thinking perhaps I would feel better when I woke, but sleeping was not an option at the moment. My skin was covered in goose-bumps, sensitive to every touch, and every wisp of air made me tingle.

Patti was right. It did come back. What did she say I should do? "Explore the feeling." I looked down at my unbound breasts and the smooth skin of my stomach. I rested my hand on my belly. *Explore the feeling.*

My nipples were tight in the cool air. I trailed my hand up and stroked one with my fingertip. A hot spark shot through my body while a shuddering sigh escaped me. I began to play with the other one as well, pinching and flicking them until they started to burn.

The throbbing between my thighs became unbearable. Tentatively, I trailed my hand down my torso to rest gently over my underwear. A massive throb took place under my hand. I began to rub gently where it felt best and quickly found a spot that made the rest of the world melt away. Suddenly, I was sure I wanted skin-on-skin. I reached under my underwear to find a greater sensation.

My senses dug up recent experiences. I felt Reid's hot breath in my ear as he whispered my name. I saw Flynn's demanding eyes as he lay in my lap. I felt Ryn's lips pressed against mine while he clutched me closer.

My stomach and leg muscles clenched as forceful waves washed over me. A moan escaped me as I shuddered repeatedly. I went limp, and a haze settled over my mind. Curling into a satisfied ball under my covers, I quickly fell asleep. My sleep was deep and undisturbed.

I awoke rested and refreshed. Stretching contently, I looked at the clock; less than two hours had passed. My mind felt like it was tucked safely in cotton. *Maybe a nice walk will help me shake off the rest of this haze.*

Getting dressed, I managed to avoid Flynn, Reid, and Ryn on my way out of the dorm. Walking aimlessly, I ended up at Peace Garden. I was sitting quietly, enjoying the sound of the brook, when I heard someone approach. It was Dane.

"I'm surprised to see you on this side of campus," I said as he walked toward me.

"This place reminds me the most of home."

I nodded in agreement.

"How is your studying coming along?" he asked.

I looked at him sharply to see if he had any ulterior motives. He looked back, merely curious and concerned.

"I am having some problems," I admitted.

"Anything I can help you with?"

"Well, I have trouble with measuring and visualization sometimes."

"Oh? Describe how you go about it."

"Like everyone else, I suppose. I still my body and open my mind. I try to measure the available magic. I feel how warm or cold the air is, how heavy it is, how it moves, and determine its frequency. Then I match my breathing. Finally, I picture what I want and let the images flow through me."

He nodded, thinking. "All of your methods are pretty conventional, except for the last. You should impose your will on the visions, not let them flow through you. You are taking command and telling the air exactly what you want it to do. It isn't a suggestion."

His advice flipped a switch in my mind, and I nodded thoughtfully.

"Try it," he suggested.

"All right."

He picked up a nearby rock the size of his fist. "Float this rock."

"But I have never been able to float anything that heavy."

"You can if you know you can."

I planted my feet and spread my fingers. The air felt...*expectant...*

High frequency. Speed up breathing. Getting near the pitch of the available magic, I opened my eyes.

"You *will* float," I told the rock. I stretched my hand out toward it, palm up. Lifting my hand, the rock rose in unison just as I told it to.

"See?" Dane encouraged. "You just have to know what you want and impose your will. You are in control." He placed his hand on my shoulder, and we smiled at each other.

"Thanks, Dane."

"It isn't long before first semester is over."

That sobered me. My two-semester, Dane-imposed time limit loomed.

"I hope you prove me wrong, Kai. But I cannot condone you wasting too much of your life in the pursuit of impossibilities. Maybe I am being selfish; I want the Kai I know back."

"I understand you are trying to save me from what you feel will be heartbreak in the end. But I really think it's possible." I pleaded for his under-standing. *I never like fighting with Dane.*

"I know, and I hope you're right. Oh, I received a strange message from Patti. Do you have any idea why she is calling me an idiot?"

I laughed. "What happens between you two is none of my business."

Dane's insight really made a difference, though sometimes my concentration was still broken by random emotions when gauging magical frequency. When I was able to concentrate, my capabilities went up exponentially. I surpassed everyone in my Air Elemental I class, except for Flynn, in a few weeks. I could even float myself.

Leif's tutoring in Magical Theory kept my grades among the top in the class.

Peace of Mind was the one class I was struggling with. Flynn and Reid were passing all their classes with flying colors, as was expected from their advanced skills. Even Leif was holding his own in his Earth Elemental I class. Though he was not bulking up like he wanted, he was considerably stronger than when he first arrived. He was also building confidence and seemed a lot more comfortable with himself.

Flynn was getting more creative with the pranks he pulled on Master Hart. Due to Reid's initial reaction, Flynn contented himself with relegating me with tales of his success rather than bringing me along.

One day at dinner, Dorm Leader called over the din of voices. "All right guys, I have news. The time has come for our yearly dorm retreat."

All the upperclassmen whooped and cheered.

"Yes, yes," he said patiently, raising his hands for silence. "This year, we are going to Gaami Temple.

Remember, this retreat is meant to help you relax before finals as well as provide you a change of scenery to practice. The monks have graciously allowed us to camp in their woodlands. This means we will be sleeping outdoors. We will also be preparing our own food. There are signup sheets in the first-floor common area. Everyone must sign up for at least one duty, be it food preparation, trash disposal, et cetera. We will be leaving Friday after dinner, so sign up and be packed before then." He motioned that he was finished, and the chatter started up again with gusto.

"How exciting!" Leif exclaimed.

"I didn't know we did a retreat," I commented.

"They ask that upperclassmen keep it a secret from the first years." Ryn smiled.

He was much more comfortable talking with us after his confession, but he did not keep his interest a secret from the group. This sometimes resulted in tension with the other guys. As for me, I was glad that I had decided not to tell him my secret. He was already obvious enough in his affections. I tried not to think about it even though he had asked me to. Knowing that I am a girl, I didn't feel I had much to think about. Though sometimes, his attentions pushed those what-if thoughts to the forefront. I had to remind myself that this was neither the time nor place for courting.

After dinner, we went to the common area to look at the duty choices. I volunteered for temple cleanup. Apparently, part of the reason the monks donated the temple woodlands for the weekend was so a group of students could help deep clean the temple. Leif signed up for food preparation. Reid went for fresh water duty. Flynn and Ryn opted for temple cleanup with me.

After much anticipation, Friday morning glowed. The excitement for the retreat was palatable. During some free time, I packed the backpack I was given for the outing. I didn't have any appropriate camping clothes, so I packed my physical training uniforms. I rolled up my provided camping blanket and stuffed in some personal hygiene products.

"Have you ever been to Gaami Temple?" I asked Flynn as he was packing.

"Sure, my parents took Reid, Ayana, and me there once."

"How do people camping bathe while there?"

"There are hot springs and..." He stopped and stared at me.

"Do people go in naked?" I asked, fearing to hear the answer.

He nodded.

I guess I won't be bathing for a few days.

Flynn stared at me anxiously.

"Don't worry," I shrugged. "I can stick it out for a couple of days."

He relaxed and nodded.

After dinner, everyone gathered outside the dorm. Carrying our packs, we marched to the front gates. Parked outside were open, animal-drawn carts. Each cart had long benches and sat about twenty people. We piled in tightly.

Our packs on our laps and sides pressed together, it wasn't a long trip to the train station. But with Flynn's body pressed against mine on one side and Ryn's on the other, the short ride seemed long and hot.

It's going to be a long *weekend.*

We arrived at the train station and learned two entire carriages had been reserved for us. Each sleeper cabin held four people. One of us had to bunk with another group.

We decided to draw for it by playing Odds or Evens. The caller, in this case me, holds one to five fingers behind his or her back. The players put their fists in a circle and say, "odds or evens." When they say "evens," everyone, including the caller, displays a number of fingers. If a player's number matches the caller's, either odd or even, the player wins. If the player's doesn't match, he or she is out.

Ryn lost. Crestfallen, he went in search of a cabin with room.

"Bye, Ryn," Flynn gloated, twinkling his fingers. "Well, shall we?" he motioned me inside.

We stored our packs in an overhead luggage rack and sat on the bench seats for a while, looking out the windows. Leif had visited the temple before, too. I listened to them tell stories about their visits. At some point, I must have fallen asleep because I woke resting my head on Reid's shoulder.

"Kai, you can have this bunk." Reid laid me down on the bench.

Flynn pulled down the bunk above me. Climbing on, he peeked over the side at me. "Night, Ki-Ki."

I smiled sleepily and wished everyone a good

night. Rolling to face the bunk across, I saw Reid's brown eyes glint at me in the low cabin-light. I wasn't sure how to interpret his expression. He stared at me intently as if trying to etch my face into his memory.

Etch my face... "Hey," I yawned. "Will you guys take a picture with me before I go home for break?"

They all agreed with enthusiasm.

I drifted off to sleep with Reid's contented smile projected in my mind. The dreams I had were steamy and involved a certain set of twins I knew.

CHAPTER 12

I awoke aching and overheated. *Where does my brain come up with this stuff? It is going to be a* very *long weekend.* Mourning my lack of alone time, I rolled over and opened my eyes. Two sets of brown eyes peered at me, one from across and one from above. Leif snored in the bunk diagonal. Images from my dream writhed to the surface.

"Did you have a bad dream, Ki-Ki?" Flynn asked, hushed.

I squinted, confused by his question.

"You were moaning," Reid clarified.

"Um...yeah, a bad dream," I lied, mumbling.

A while later, a train steward brought sweet rolls for breakfast. I woke Leif, and we folded the upper bunks. It wasn't long before the train stopped, and we piled out onto Gaami platform. Ryn soon rejoined us.

"Did you sleep well?" he asked me solicitously. "I missed you," he added. That last comment earned him a knock upside the head from Reid.

It looks like Reid is on Ryn duty today.

Our morning physical training consisted of hiking all the way to Gaami Temple. Gaami Temple was imposing, with a triangular roof and columns all around the base to hold it up. There were no walls, just pillars. Carved into the roof were the Seven High Deities: Hest, the god of fire; Borus, the god of Air; Permetia, the goddess of water; Ina, the goddess of earth; Avella, the goddess of birth; Caal, the god of death; and Heldan, the goddess of afterlife.

Monks went about their chores. The head monk waited for us on the front steps. He welcomed us and told Dorm Leader where our camping site was. Dorm Leader thanked him and promised some of us would return later to clean the temple.

We hiked to our campsite, and the group that signed up for setup duty started to work. The fire starters made campfires, and Leif and others began making lunch. Reid went to collect fresh water from a spring not far away. The temple cleaning crew joined the water crew to fill our cleaning buckets so we could clean the temple after lunch.

The spring was cool and clear. Little fish swam around happily.

Returning to camp, some of us rested while lunch was being prepared.

After a delicious lunch, Flynn, Ryn, and I, along with the rest of the temple cleaning crew, grabbed our buckets and rags and walked to the temple.

A group of monks directed us where to clean. They were particularly pleased that there were air and water users among the group as water users could direct the water anywhere and air users could float to the roof to clean.

Floating while washing was exhausting. After all the dust and grime had been washed away, a water fight broke out. The monks looked on, smiling indulgently at our youthful exuberance. A few even joined in.

Taking cover behind a pillar, I noticed Reid walking around the building. Having already dumped a bucket of water on Flynn, I decided it was time for Reid's payback as well. I crept behind him, silently stalking him like prey. He stopped in a thicket of trees and removed his shoes.

He must be out here to practice. Now is my chance.

I floated into a tree with my bucket. Climbing out on a limb, I held the bucket over his head. His eyes were closed. He was completely vulnerable. I turned the bucket over, and he stepped to the side. Not a drop hit him.

"Did you think I couldn't hear you? Come on, *Flynn* is my brother." He laughed up at me.

Putting my hands on my hips to deliver a smart retort, I lost my balance. I tensed for impact. Gravity was faster than my reflexes, but not Reid's. He moved to catch me.

Releasing the tension in my limbs, I mentally checked for injuries. Everything was in order. I opened my eyes and discovered I was nose-to-nose with Reid. In a collision of limbs, he had landed on his back, and I was on top of him. His arms grasped me tightly, protecting me from the hard ground.

"Are you all right?" I whispered.

"I'm fine," he whispered back.

I sighed in relief. That is when I felt the full force of my body pressed against his. The throbbing slammed my core. I could feel Reid's hot breath on my mouth. *I should probably move...*I started to wiggle free, but his arms tightened.

"Wait," he said, looking like he was concentrating.

"Why?" I breathed. *Is he hurt after all?* I mentally took stock of all his body parts that were touching mine to make sure nothing was bent in an unnatural angle.

I felt something very out of the ordinary. A hard lump shuddered into my upper thigh. As it jumped, it dug into me painfully. I recalled a discussion Charlotte had with me when I became of a marriageable age. At the time, the marriage bed felt far away and kind of scared me.

It didn't feel so far away now as Reid tried to collect himself. The hard lump jumped against my thigh again, sending a hot shiver through my body, and I wasn't scared. My response to him made Reid gasp and close his eyes.

"This is difficult," he ground out. Trying to give us some relief, I instructed him to loosen his arms. Concentrating with all I had, I floated away from him. *Maybe this was why Flynn ran away that time.*

Reid stood carefully and brushed himself off. Looking up at me, he must have seen my desire had not waned. If anything, the distance between our bodies had made it worse.

Wearing the same painful expression I had seen

on Flynn, he excused himself and left to walk it off. I was left alone to figure out what to do with the desire gnawing at me.

Determined to run it off, I plunged deeper into the woods. But no matter how hard I ran, I couldn't get rid of the feeling of Reid pressed against me. I found a secluded clump of trees and took care of it. I felt refreshed as I walked toward the temple, contemplating what this meant for Reid's and my friendship.

Will he want to pretend it didn't happen like Flynn? Or pursue it like Ryn? He knows I am a girl so that isn't a problem. But to others, it would look like he prefers men.

Approaching the temple, I happened upon a monk who was replacing offerings on an altar to Hest.

"Merrily met, Searcher." I extended my arm to the monk.

"Merrily met." He smiled and grasped my forearm.

"Can I help?"

"Of course."

I helped the monk arrange flowers, fruits, and incense on the altar. When we were finished, we shared a cup of cool tea.

"How goes your studying, Searcher?" he asked. I told him about my problem with gauging magical frequency.

"It sounds like you have too much empathy."

"What do you mean?"

He just smiled a smile that told me that was all I

would get. Sitting companionably, I contemplated what he had said.

Eventually, inspiration struck me like a club to the head. *Thank you, Hest!* I thanked the monk and rushed back to camp.

"May the Seven bless you, Searcher," he called after me.

While eating dinner, my head was full of possibilities. I didn't hear Flynn's question the first time.

"Have you seen Reid?" he repeated.

"He isn't here?" I flushed when Reid was nowhere in sight.

"I hope he is all right," Flynn worried.

I vowed to find him.

We began our search immediately after dinner, taking handlights in case we didn't find him before the dimming. We split up, each taking a direction. Hours passed as we called and searched. Anyone who found him was supposed to return to camp and have a fire user send up a flare. The dimming was underway when I came upon a glade. Leaning on a tree next to a spring, Reid stared at his reflection.

"Reid, I am so glad you are safe." I dropped down next to him.

He looked at me, surprised by my sudden appearance. He had not comprehended my words. He searched my face for something. "I love you." He sounded surprised by his admission. Taking my hand, his eyes pleaded with me to understand. "But I respect your quest, and I do not want to jeopardize it. I know how much it means to you. Now is not the time to pursue my feelings, but I want you to know I will nurture them until the time is right."

My heart pounded, and I was unsure of the correct response. "Thank you, Reid."

We returned to camp and sent up a flare. Flynn returned like a whirlwind. He berated his brother's thoughtlessness, and Reid took it, knowing he was at fault.

We rolled out our blankets. I slept between Leif and Reid. Flynn slept closely to Reid, reassuring himself that his twin was safe.

The morning glowed, and we had breakfast after physical training. Then we all split to find good places to practice. I returned to the glade Reid had found the day before.

Standing in the center, I opened myself to the magical frequency.

...tranquility...

When Magic's emotion surfaced this time, I was ready. Rather than fight it for my concentration, I let it wash over me. I let the tranquility take control of my emotions. It seeped deep into my muscles and bones until I was as loose as water.

I slowed my breathing to match. The perfect pitch. In complete harmony, I then imposed my will as if saying: "I see you. I know you. I feel what you feel. Trust me and follow my lead."

I shot into the air, not floating but flying, telling the air to carry me wherever I wanted to go. I flew above the treetops, the wind blowing my hair away from my face. I reveled in the freedom and the thrill of working together with Magic as one. I flew around, looking for Flynn, and found him in a clearing like the one I had left. I called to him and he looked up at me, shocked. I landed softly not three feet from him.

I closed my eyes and thanked Magic for working with me. Then I released it to do its will. I asked the Seven to bless the Searcher who had given me the key.

I never thought I would see Flynn speechless. I grinned and winked at him as he had taught me.

"How...?" He stared, awestruck.

I explained how I had been distracted by emotions, the monk's observation, and what I did to embrace those emotions. My explanation seemed to confuse him more.

"Emotions? I never felt any emotions while gauging magic. I just use the physical indicators like movement and humidity."

I shrugged. "Well, that's what I did."

"Have you figured out how to create air yet?"

I sighed. "That is the next step."

"You'll get it. Show me again!" he demanded excitedly.

I flew around the clearing again as he smiled up at me.

With a look of determination, he asked to be alone to practice.

"Good luck," I called, flying back to the glade. Landing, I thanked and released Magic. I was planning to meditate on how to create air, but the tinkling of the spring beckoned to me. *I think I will reward myself with a quick bath.*

CHAPTER 13

The water was cool and refreshing. I didn't have any soap, but I was able to soak the sweat off. Getting out, I returned to the tree where I had left my clothes and found them gone.

"My eyes must be blessed, for I see a nymph." Des stepped out from behind the tree, holding my clothes. I reached to snatch them, but he was too fast. "Well, well, *Kie*. I knew there was something different about you."

"Give me the clothes, Des."

"And what will I get in return?"

"How about I will *not* punch you in the face?"

"Tsk, tsk, that's not the way for a lady to behave. My father is on the university board, you know. How about I let your little secret slip the next time I see him?"

I sighed, defeated. "Anything you want, but let me get dressed."

He threw me the clothes and turned his back

politely, like he hadn't seen it all already. I cleared my throat to indicate when I was clothed.

"So what do you want?"

"That remains to be seen. Tell me, does my brother know you are a woman?"

"No," I said through clenched teeth.

"Now, that *is* interesting. He has been fawning over you these past weeks thinking you were a man? Oh yes, this could be *very* fun."

His smile made my stomach curdle and my skin crawl.

"You needn't worry. I will keep your secret, for now. But be sure you stay in touch." He ran his forefinger along my jaw, where Ryn had trailed his lips weeks before.

I shuddered.

He slithered away to whatever dank hole he had crawled out of.

I rushed back to camp in search of Leif, Flynn, and Reid. They looked nauseated when I told them what had happened.

"What do we do?" Leif asked after a pensive silence.

"I guess, we wait," I said.

Flynn and Reid looked both disgusted and infuriated.

Ryn walked up and placed his arm around my shoulders. "What's going on, guys?"

Flynn and Reid just stared at him, not even censuring him for his proximity to me. I cast my eyes down.

Leif salvaged the situation. "Did you hear, Ryn? Kie was able to fly today."

"That's great! Then why is everyone so down?"

"Because he still can't make air."

"Well, that's all right, Kie." He consoled me by rubbing my back. "You have plenty of time. You'll get it."

After lunch, I tried to practice more, but I couldn't get into it. I just watched Ryn as he was the only one not distracted. Me watching him seemed to give him pleasure. I let him have it since I didn't know what would happen in the days to come.

After dinner, we hiked back to the train station. This time, Leif voluntarily gave up his bunk to Ryn. Ryn didn't care why. He was so pleased. Sitting much closer to me than was necessary, he was overjoyed that I didn't move away, and Flynn and Reid didn't strike him. The return trip was solemn; only Ryn enjoyed it.

The next morning, we were served sweet rolls again. When we arrived at Capital Station, no carts awaited us. "Because we missed physical training this morning, we will walk," Dorm Leader told us cheerfully.

We returned to the dorm with just enough time to shower and change before classes. First term was rapidly coming to a close, and everyone was studying for finals as well as making plans for break. We had been anxious for weeks, not knowing when Des would strike.

After breakfast one morning, I returned to my room to find a letter chip in an envelope under my door. Putting the chip in my RWD, I saw it was a letter from Patti, or rather an invitation. She invited me as well as Flynn, Reid, Leif, and Ryn to a ball at Madame Bergot's. It was on the Saturday that break started. At the bottom, there was a special note for me to come early. "And don't worry about formal wear for you. I will whip up something handsome for you."

Thanks, Patti. She knows I don't have any formal men's clothes.

I told everyone at lunch about the ball. Leif was very excited. Flynn, Reid, and Ryn reluctantly agreed to go.

"But I won't be able to dance with *you*, Kie," Ryn complained.

"But there will be plenty of pretty *girls* for you to dance with," Leif promised.

Ryn grunted acknowledgement.

"Come on, guys. It will be our last hoorah before break," I encouraged.

"That reminds me," Ryn said. "What are you doing for break?"

We all said we were going home. Ryn looked downtrodden by the news. Leif promised to visit Ryn during break since his family also lived in Capital.

Flynn had a mischievous glint in his eyes that I did not care to pursue the meaning of.

Ryn was a little cheered by Leif's promise until he noticed Des hovering nearby. Des caught my attention and beckoned me to follow him. Ryn was astonished when I followed Des to the common area.

"I have decided what I want from you, sweet nymph," Des said quietly.

"I'm listening."

"Before break, I want you to crush my brother's heart."

CHAPTER 14

I passed my finals with top marks. I even got a higher score than Flynn on our Air Elemental I final. It was a relief that we were all allowed to continue into next term. I waited until after finals to carry out Des's blackmail as I didn't want the upset to mess with Ryn's scores.

The night before the ball, I invited Ryn on a walk. He bounced with excitement at the special attention. We strolled into the trees behind the dorm where no one could hear us.

"At your request, I have thought it over," I said, turning to Ryn seriously.

"I am so glad to hear…"

"There is no hope, Ryn. As a man, I cannot be with another man," I asserted in a non-negotiable tone.

He looked like I had slapped him. "Oh," he breathed.

I excused myself and ran back to the dorm without looking back. Sprinting to my room, at least

I got inside before I burst into tears at the pain I had caused. I rushed at Flynn and buried my face in his chest, explaining what I had done in between sobs. He rocked me until I was finished and tucked me into my bunk. Not wanting to be alone, I grabbed onto his shirt as he moved away from my bed.

"Don't leave me," I whimpered.

He looked unsure at first, then made a scooching motion. I made room for him as he climbed into my bed. He tucked me safely under his arm with my head on his chest. I slept soundly as he stroked my hair.

I awoke and snuggled closer to Flynn's spicy scent. Still drowsy, I wrapped my arm around his torso and dragged my thigh up his leg. A responsive hardness answered my inner thigh.

Okay! I am awake. I bolted upright and looked at Flynn. He stared at me, frightened.

"Flynn, I'm sorry. I didn't think about how this might affect you. I just didn't want to be alone after—"

He cleared his throat and tried to look diplomatic. "It's all right. *Nothing happened.*" He climbed slowly out of my bunk.

"I am truly sorry," I whispered.

"Bathroom," he managed.

I felt ashamed of what I had done to Flynn. After all, I knew what that throbbing need demanded. *And he knows I am a girl...His self-restraint in the face of my zeal is incredible.*

Recalling his spicy scent and his hardness on my thigh, I got excited all over. I snuck up to the bathroom door to try to estimate how long Flynn would be in there. Pressing my ear to the wood, I heard a repetitive wet sound and Flynn moaning.

The sounds he made had me nearing my own peak. I leaned my back against the bathroom door and rubbed in time with the wet sound. It took everything I had not to make noise as we climaxed together.

When Flynn opened the door, I fell backward. He caught me before I hit the floor.

"What...?" Mortification overtook his expression. "Did you hear...?"

"*Something* happened," I responded seriously. He lit up red with embarrassment.

"Why are you embarrassed?" I was genuinely confused. *I thought this sort of self-maintenance was normal. Patti told me about it without being embarrassed.*

"Because," he said like that was an explanation.

"Doesn't everybody?" I asked. "Isn't it normal?"

"I assume so, yes. But..."

"Then why are you embarrassed? I am not embarrassed."

"You mean you..."

"Yes, the sounds you were making were quite exciting." I said it as a compliment.

He looked like the idea of me participating made him excited. "They were?" He seemed pleased.

"Yes, Patti didn't tell me about that. I wonder if she knows. She told me to be alone, so maybe she doesn't. It was much better with you. Will you do it again with me next time?"

"You mean, you want... to watch each other?"

"No, I am fairly clear on the fact that we aren't supposed to see the opposite sex unclothed before marriage. But I don't see anything wrong with hearing each other do something everyone does anyway."

He considered this possibility like it was a revolutionary idea. "I suppose you are right. It really is no different from anything else you do every day. We don't get embarrassed about brushing our teeth or hair. And as long as I don't see or touch you, you will not be shamed."

"Exactly." I smiled at the prospect.

"But let's keep it between us roommates, shall we?"

"Why is that?"

"Because I don't want other...because it is implausible for you to go to other people's rooms all the time. You wouldn't go to someone else's room to take a shower, would you?"

"I see your point. You know, I had no idea men had to do this, too."

"Really? I had no idea women did."

"But sometimes it is inconvenient. Sometimes, I want it again right after I just finished."

He stared at me. "Well, I will try to accommodate that."

Over break we were still supposed to do physical training, so Flynn and I went for a run. Then we met the others for breakfast. Ryn looked miserable, and Des was enjoying it.

"Are you not feeling well, Ryn?" Leif asked.

Ryn shook his head.

"Are you going to skip the ball then?"

"No…" His eyes flicked to me, and he looked nauseous. "I'm still going."

Everyone agreed to meet after lunch to go to Madame Bergot's.

It seemed they were all determined to be as attractive as possible for the ball, especially Ryn. I alone wore a plain, boring suit.

We took the trolley to a stop near Madame Bergot's and walked to the school. It was all decked out and sparkly. The doorman looked at my suit disdainfully. The ballroom was further back, past a grand staircase and a number of closed doors.

On the way to the ballroom to look for Patti, someone snatched my hand and dragged me into one of the rooms off the hall. Patti shut the door behind us. We stood alone in a small music room with the lights turned out.

"Hurry and change." She threw a bundle of cloth at me.

I entered the ballroom self-consciously. *I never thought this is what she had planned.*

Flynn was the closest and the first to see me. His eyes were huge when he took in my shimmering green dress. The wig I wore was the exact color and style of my hair before I had cut it.

"Ki-Ki…uh Ms. Stephenson, you look wonderful," Flynn bowed over my hand. "I have to say, I prefer you as a girl," he whispered so only I could hear.

Patti found Leif, and they both appeared very

pleased to be reunited. I approached them on Flynn's arm.

"May I present Ms. Stephenson?" Flynn said to Leif proudly.

Leif smiled so wide I thought his cheeks would split. "It is so nice to *finally* meet the beautiful Ms. Stephenson," he said, taking my hand.

Flynn brought me to Reid next. "Dear brother, I know *you* have been anxious to meet Ms. Stephenson."

Reid stepped close and took my hand. "Ms. Stephenson," he pronounced reverently. Then he turned my hand over and kissed my palm, a sign to all other men that he would pursue courting me. His eyes captured mine. "May I have the first dance?"

"Y-yes, of course," I breathed, dumbstruck. He pulled me toward him as the music started.

"I thought you were going to wait to pursue me?" I whispered as we spun around the floor.

"Hmm...well, that was before I saw every other man in the room staring at you. I will try my best to woo you only when you are openly a woman. Is that a fair compromise?"

"I suppose it's fair."

He pulled me closer, continuing to dance proficiently. As we danced, I saw Ms. Shale talking with Ryn. I had vowed to try to avoid Ryn since changing my clothes as he might recognize me. However, the dance movements brought us close enough to hear their conversation.

"I was so sure you were going to bring Mr.

Stephenson with you, Mr. Breshire." Ms. Shale expressed her disappointment.

"We did." He looked around to point me out to Ms. Shale. We made brief eye contact before Reid spun me away. Ryn pursued us and insisted on cutting in. Reid had no choice but to allow it. Ryn and I danced the remainder of the song in silence. He just stared at me with an indecipherable expression. His wide, brown eyes searched my face for answers. As the song closed, he led me to the patio through opened glass doors.

"K-Kie?" he said finally.

"Kai, actually. Kai Stephenson. It is nice to make your acquaintance, Mr. Breshire."

"You are a woman."

"Yes."

He stared at me, and I waited for his anger to fall on me. It never came. He sighed and smiled wider and happier than I had ever seen him.

"You aren't angry?"

"Angry? I have never been so happy in my life."

"But Ryn, you can't tell anyone," I hushed.

"Obviously, you would get thrown out of school." His tone was so matter-of-fact that I burst into a hysterical fit of laughter. After I quieted, he turned to me seriously.

"Do you stand by what you said before?"

"What's that?"

"You said, 'as a man, I cannot be with another man.'"

"Yes."

"Wonderful!" He grabbed my hand and pulled

me back toward the ballroom. Turning my hand over, he kissed my palm in full view of everyone there. Reid looked less than pleased and seemed to take it as a personal challenge, which I supposed it was.

With two suitors already stating their intentions so publically, no one else asked me to dance besides Flynn and Leif.

Leif seemed a little upset as we moved around the floor in graceful circles.

"What's wrong, Leif?" I asked.

"I'm sorry, Kai," he said miserably.

"Why?" My concern bordered on alarm.

"I feel terrible. I think I really like Ms. Nord, but I already promised to marry you."

I laughed so hard that we had to stop dancing because I was messing up the steps. My sides began to hurt, and I could hardly breathe.

Leif didn't know how to react to my outburst. Eventually, I caught my breath and said, "That's all right, Leif. Just don't tell anyone what you saw, okay? And, just so you know, I think Patti likes you, too."

It was adorable how relieved and happy he was at my response.

While taking a break from dancing and waiting for Ryn to bring me punch, I noticed a flash of light coming from a room off the hallway. Exploring the flash, I discovered a photographer was taking portraits of guests.

Excited, I gathered Flynn, Reid, Leif, and Ryn together and begged for a portrait. They readily agreed under the provision they each got a copy. We grouped together for the portrait when it was our turn. I stood in front, and Flynn and Reid stood behind me, their faces towered over my shoulders. Leif stood at Reid's side and Ryn at Flynn's.

We asked the photographer's assistant to make four additional copies of the negative chip. We each left the room with a treasure. I couldn't wait to see it in my picture stand.

The rest of the night flew in a flurry of shimmering skirts. It was so nice not to have to hide my true sex for once, to be openly female in public. I hadn't realized how exhausting it was to hide my femininity, and I never thought I would miss being a woman. It was over too quickly. I changed back into my suit, which was definitely more comfortable, and promised to see Patti on the train home the following day.

We took the trolley back to the university. After packing my suitcase, I lay in bed replaying the evening in my head.

"You really are beautiful," Flynn whispered in the dark.

"Thank you, Flynn. You are beautiful too." I was asleep before I heard his response.

CHAPTER 15

When I opened my eyes the next morning, Flynn was staring at me from over the edge of my bunk, not four inches from my face.

"Ki-Ki, since we won't be roommates for a couple of weeks, can we fulfill our maintenance before you leave?"

The thought of yesterday morning sent a shiver through me. Images from the dream I had about Flynn and Reid on the train to Gaami flashed in my mind.

"I think I need that."

In order to hear each other better, we left the bathroom door cracked. We both leaned against the wall close to the door, him in the bathroom and me in the bedroom.

Since he knew I was there, I didn't try to be quiet. I matched the speed of my rubbing to the speed of his wet sounds again. Our moans seemed to feed each other. His sounds of pleasure sent hot shivers through me.

I peaked before him, but the sounds of his continued gratification had me ready to go again. When he finally climaxed, we peaked together.

We slumped, spent, on either side of the wall for a while. Fuzzy-headed and sluggish, I finally managed to stand on shaky legs.

"Flynn?" I whispered. He grunted in response.

"Are you all right?"

"Are you joking?" he laughed. "I feel like I could never do it again."

"Well, don't say *that*," I urged playfully.

"You keep using that tone, and you will miss your train."

I had more than enough time to catch my train, so I stopped at a bakery and bought a basket of raspberry tarts on the way to the station. I boarded my train without incident and located the cabin Patti and I shared. We closed the curtains, and I changed into a dress and put on the wig. Patti gushed about the night before. In reality, she gushed about Leif. Before long, Dane found his way into our cabin.

"Sorry I am late," he kissed his sister on the cheek and bent over my hand. He looked pleased to see me as a girl again.

"How is it that Kai got here before you?" Patti asked.

Dane took her nagging good-naturedly as always.

Now that her brother had joined the party, Patti toned down her enthusiasm about Leif. She told me all about school and the friends she had made there. Dane tuned her out and read a bookchip on his RWD. When she brought up the Jamisons' annual Tree Day ball, his eyes stopped following the page.

"Will you be attending again this year?" Patti asked me.

"I suppose, though I don't look forward to being chased by Charles Jamison yet again."

"Everyone knows Charlie has been after you since we were all ten. Just rely on Dane like you did last year. You don't mind, do you, Brother?"

Dane's face reddened. "If I can be of assistance..."

"But Patti, Dane doesn't want to have to look after me all night. I am sure he would rather be courting someone, Scarlet Winter, for instance," I added suggestively.

Dane's lips pressed into a line.

"Oh Kai, don't tease him! You know Scarlet only chases him because Charlie pays attention to you."

"I'm sorry, Dane. I couldn't help but tease you a little."

"Long-suffering is a phrase that comes to mind." He smiled back at me.

"Why don't you two just get married already? Then Kai and I could really be sisters," Patti said for the millionth time in our lives.

"Patti! That was funny when we were young, but we are of marriageable ages now. What if someone who fancies Dane heard you?"

Dane turned off his RWD and rose to leave, asking if we wanted anything from the dining car.

The next three days passed similarly. Patti and I

chatted. Sometimes, we teased Dane. He really was a good sport.

The train stopped at many stations along the way. The scenery outside the window went from city to country to town to county and so on. We eventually reached the end of the line, Sweet Water. Our little town consisted of a main street with necessities and not much else.

The Nord family's coachman was there to pick us up at the station. As my house was on the way to theirs, they graciously gave me a ride. I promised to visit Patti the next day after I had settled in, and I thanked Dane for escorting us.

My home was not large, but it was not small either. We had a lot of land as well as stables and horses, but we did not have blue shard-powered lights. Our staff included a housekeeper, a cook, a maid, and a groom.

Our maid, Stella, must have heard the carriage pull up because she was there to open the door for me.

"Miss Kai, welcome home!" She hugged me, excited.

"Thank you, Stella. How is everyone?"

"Your mother and father are well and the same as when you left, Miss. Mable is as hearty as ever. She is making your favorite for dinner. Bram got thrown a while back, but he has recovered nicely. He was always a chipper lad. And Miss Charlotte is holding down the fort, trying her best as usual."

I nodded. "And how are you, Stella?"

"Oh, I am well, Miss. Glad you are home safe and sound."

"Where is my mother?"

"She is in her studio, Miss."

"Thank you, Stella."

She took my suitcase to my room, and I walked to the back of the house.

My mother was a great artist, for a woman, that is. As most well-born women, she was expected to study something artistic. She excelled at drawing with charcoal. My father had built her a studio when they were first married. The back wall was made of windows.

Entering the brightly-lit room, I saw my mother on the window seat with her sketchbook. Her fingers were black with coal as dark as the hair I had inherited from her, and she had some smudged on her cheek as well. She did not look up when I entered.

"I'm home, Mother," I said, wiping the smudge off her cheek and kissing it.

"Oh, hello, Dear. Are you back so soon? Please tell Charlotte I am running out of paper again. Will you, Dear?"

"Of course, Mother." She did not look away from her drawing at all.

I left the house from the back door and walked toward the stables. Bram saw me coming and scooped me into a spinning hug.

"Miss Kai! Well, don't you just get prettier every time I see you?"

"Thank you, Bram. How are you feeling? I heard you were thrown."

"Oh, don't you worry about that, Miss. I am plenty healthy. Your father is in with Pandit if you want to see him."

I nodded and entered the stables. Just as Bram said, Father was tending to Pandit, brushing him and cleaning his hooves.

"Father, I am home," I said quietly.

"Hush, Girl. You will spook him," my father snapped. Pandit swished his tail and inched toward me. Stroking Pandit's soft nose, I tried again.

"How are you, Father?" I asked in a hushed tone.

"If you can't grab a brush and be quiet, go somewhere else."

I picked up a brush and gently combed Pandit's mane. Feeling like I fulfilled my obligations, I went in search of Charlotte.

Charlotte was in the study, going over the monthly expenses. I knocked gently on the door and entered. She looked up, and a warm smile broke on her face.

"Kai, my girl, you are finally home!" She rose from the desk and hurried to embrace me. "Let me look at you, Miss Fancy Finishing School."

A guilty pang followed that comment. I smiled and reveled in her warm welcome and petting.

She had Stella bring us tea.

"How are you, Charlotte?"

"We are all getting along just fine here. But you tell me all about the big city and what you learned at school."

It was lucky for me Patti had just spent the last three days talking about school. I felt so guilty lying to Charlotte, but I didn't see a better way. She listened intently to everything I said.

After tea and a chat with Charlotte, I went to the kitchen to see Mable. As always, she was covered in flour. So instead of a hug, I settled for kissing her on the cheek.

"I am making your favorite stew for dinner tonight," she promised.

"You are the best, Mable."

After a short talk with her about her health and happiness, I left the house to go to Sei. Through the woods in a little grove was Sei's house, quaint and modest but warm and welcoming.

Armed with apology tarts from the best bakery in Capital, I entered Sei's house without knocking. He sat hunched in a rocking chair by the fire, whittling a wooden flute.

"Your favorite student has brought you a treat," I said, placing the basket of tarts on the table.

"*My* favorite student would write me like she promised," he retorted grumpily.

"So the tarts double as a bribe." I smiled my winning smile that always won him over.

He stared at me stone-faced. We were at an impasse. After a few drawn-out seconds, he smiled warmly.

"So the wandering lass has come home? Come here, Girl," he said, opening his arms. I stepped into his welcoming embrace. Bringing him a tart, I sat in the other chair by the fireplace.

"So what did you learn?" he asked excitedly.

I told him all about my classes and my lessons

with Ichii and Roan. I told him about Dane's insight and the monk that gave me the key.

"Empathy, huh?" he considered that, nodding.

He chuckled and slapped his knee when I described how high and fast I flew, but he did not look worried that I hadn't figured out how to make air yet.

"You will, my girl. You are almost there. I can feel it."

Finally, I told him about Dane's deadline.

"That closed-minded, addle-brained fool; I always knew he was trouble. But don't you worry. You learn faster and work harder than any student I have ever had. You will show that puppy."

After my oration, and leaving a great many personal experiences out, Sei wanted to see what I could do. We walked outside to find three familiar faces in his backyard. Reid was weeding his garden, Leif was scrubbing his walk, and Flynn was chopping wood. Shocked, I looked at Sei. He was wearing a sly grin.

"I had to have some way of keeping up with you since you never write. These nice boys have been writing to me about your progress. So how could I refuse when they wanted to visit on break?"

"Sorry, Kai." Leif looked sheepish.

"Leif, you?"

"Well, you mentioned that you studied with Master Sei, so I wrote to him to gauge your knowledge and try to help. He wrote back asking how you were. But the whole idea of visiting you was Flynn's doing."

"Of course, it was," I mumbled. Shock over, I was relieved to have my friends near me. I smiled openly at each of them.

"And the first thing you did was put them to work?" I laughed at Sei.

He shrugged. "I'm just an old man, and they are such able-bodied, strong lads," he said pitifully.

"Yeah right, I see you boys fell for it."

"Show me what you can do, Girl," Sei encouraged, unwilling to wait any longer.

I flew around his backyard and floated various things, including Flynn, who had looked just too smug about his little surprise. Sei was impressed and praised my progress, which was a much better reward than a passing exam grade.

After a while, I heard Mable whistle to warn me that dinner was almost ready. I promised to see them the next day and rushed home to wash for dinner. Dinner was quiet and had the air of necessity.

Afterward, I went upstairs and entered the first door on the left, Toby's room. It was the same as always, just as he had left it. But there was no dust, a sign that Mother still insisted Stella keep it clean.

Sighing, I shut the door and went to my room. I lit the candle on my bedside table and changed into a nightgown.

I picked up my picture stand and flipped the switch. An image of Toby and I on his birthday was projected from the stand. He smiled brightly as he clutched a stuffed dog that I had saved my allowance for months to get for him. It wore a brilliant satin ribbon of sapphire-blue around its neck, the same color as my eyes.

Remembering my newest picture chip, I dug through my luggage and found the picture chip from the ball.

Removing Toby's chip and placing it safely in a drawer, I put in the newer one. A picture of Flynn, Reid, Leif, Ryn, and me was projected. They looked so nice dressed formally and smiling. I did not even look like myself. I was sparkling with excitement. We looked like a faerie court.

I smiled at Flynn's grinning face. *I can't believe you brought everyone all this way. You always seem to know exactly what I need.*

I turned the stand off and climbed into bed. Blowing out the candle, I lay awake in the familiar room, missing "home" and the comforting sound of Flynn's even breathing.

I awoke early the next morning before the glowing at my usual time, way before a lady should be awake. The rest of the household would be asleep for hours.

I put on a dress that was easy to move in and snuck out of the house. Using a handlight, I found that Flynn, Reid, and Leif were up at Sei's as well, stretching for physical training.

Sei worked us way harder than Master Graham. Even Flynn and Reid were beat.

They all agreed to visit Patti with me that day though Leif was the most enthusiastic about the proposition.

Sneaking back into the house, I was washed and

changed before Stella came to fetch me for breakfast. Breakfast was much like dinner the night before, quiet and necessary. I felt sorry for Mable. Her food was so delicious, and my parents did not look like they even tasted it.

Wearing my best visiting dress, I went to Sei's to collect the boys. Flynn and Reid looked tickled. "Will we get to see you dressed like that every day, Ms. Stephenson?" Flynn asked.

"Why, Mr. Williams! Do you suppose to see me every day?"

"Indeed, I do. For as long as possible."

I blushed in response, surprised and pleased by his unexpected affection.

We started the moderate walk to the Nords'.

CHAPTER 16

"Good morning, James," I said politely to the Nords' butler, "Are Patti and Dane available?"

"Yes, Ms. Stephenson." He showed us to the drawing room.

"James, how many times do I have to tell you to call me Kai?"

"Of course, Miss."

I loved teasing James. He was so formal compared to our staff.

Dane entered first, confused when told he had visitors. He dropped the RWD he was carrying in the doorway when he saw Flynn, Reid, and Leif.

"What are *you* doing here?" he demanded, his eyes focused on Flynn.

"Oh, come now, old boy, aren't you happy to see your schoolmates? We came all this way to see you," Flynn said, shocked.

"I very much doubt that," he snorted.

"Now, now. There is a lady present." Flynn motioned to me.

"My apologies, Ms. Stephenson." Dane crossed the room and took my hand, holding it longer than was proper. The other men shifted restlessly.

"Kai, what is this I hear about visitors...?" Patti entered the room. "Why, Leif and the Mr. Williamses! What a pleasant surprise."

They greeted Patti properly, and she rang James for tea. We sat quietly drinking tea as Patti acted as hostess and asked about their journeys.

Come to think of it, they must have been on the same train as us.

"Leif, will you be attending the Jamisons' ball?" Patti asked innocently.

"I have not been invited."

"Not to worry. The ball is open to all who are in town. Kai and I will both be attending."

"Well in that case, of course I will attend."

"Mr. Flynn and Mr. Reid, will you attend as well?"

Dane scowled at his sister.

"*Thank you*, Ms. Nord. We would be delighted. I hope you will dance with us like last time, Ms. Stephenson," Flynn said directly to Dane.

"I have promised to attend with Mr. Nord, but I am sure he will not begrudge you a few dances." I looked at Dane.

He appeared to mind very much.

I guess he is worried about Scarlet Winter.

"Might I point out that I have already stated my

intentions toward Ms. Stephenson at a public gathering. This entitles me to some time with her, if she is willing, with chaperones present," Reid said matter-of-factly.

Dane looked like Reid had punched him in the gut. "You have stated your intentions? When?" he demanded.

"At the ball at Madame Bergot's, and I was not the only one."

"Who...?" Dane's eyes slid to Flynn, who held up his hands.

"Not I. Ryn Breshire."

Patti stepped in before our gathering could get any more heated. "That's settled. Dane, you will escort Ms. Stephenson to the ball, but allow Mr. Reid his allotted time, should she approve it." She raised her eyebrows at me, and I nodded. "I will help you with Ms. Winter when Ms. Stephenson is unavailable."

"But Ms. Nord, don't you have an escort?" Leif asked.

"I do not, Leif."

"Well then, please allow me."

Patti readily accepted, and I smiled at the pair of them. *It is nice to see Leif so confident and Patti so happy.*

"I guess that just leaves little old me," Flynn said dramatically. "Maybe I will like this Ms. Winter."

My stomach unexpectedly bottomed out. I put my teacup in its saucer, not able to handle its sudden bitterness.

"Go for it," Dane encouraged.

"Let's walk into town, shall we? I need to purchase sketch paper." I popped out of my chair, needing to move.

Patti was not keen on walking, and Leif wanted to stay with her. Propriety dictated that Dane stay as well to act as chaperone.

Flynn, Reid, and I took our leave and promised to collect Leif later. The walk to town was quite a hike. As we were used to physical exercise, it was not a problem. A bell tinkled above us as we entered the bookstore. While most of the store was bookchips and RWDs, there were some art supplies as well.

"Welcome, Ms. Stephenson. Here to purchase sketch paper for your mother?" the man behind the counter asked, eyeing Flynn and Reid.

"Yes, Ralph. Thank you."

Having obtained my mother's paper, I showed Flynn and Reid around our small town. At the end of the street was the train station. The train had just stopped, and its bell still rang to announce its arrival. Everyone about town paused to see who was arriving as it was big news to have visitors.

Ryn stepped onto the platform and waved when he spotted us. Flynn and Reid looked as astonished as I felt.

"I didn't think finding you would be so easy." He grinned as he approached.

"How did you find us at all?" Flynn wondered.

"Leif wrote to apologize that he would be unable to visit during break."

Poor Leif. Flynn looks like murder.

"Where are you staying?" Reid asked suspiciously.

"At the inn. There is only one. Where else would I stay?"

No one answered.

"Well, Mr. Breshire, I hope you will join us at the Jamisons' ball?"

Flynn's and Reid's heads snapped in my direction.

"Did someone say ball?" Des stepped off the train.

Ryn looked horrified. Reid matched Flynn's murderous expression. *Des, in my hometown?*

"Hello, Ms. Stephenson. It is a *pleasure* to see you again." Des grabbed my hand, and I resisted the urge to snatch it away rudely.

"When have you seen her before?" Ryn asked.

"I have seen more of her than you could ever hope for. Which reminds me, I believe we had an agreement, Ms. Stephenson?"

I started to quiver, and he stepped closer to me menacingly.

Ryn pulled him away. "What have you seen, Des?"

Des smirked. "Enough to shame her into an unmarriageable state," he said so only our small group could hear.

A fist crunched into Des's face. Flynn's knuckles dripped blood as he clenched his hand and stood over Des's prostrated form. Reid looked the most shocked at Flynn's display of aggression.

"Nothing you could ever do to her would shame her in that way," Flynn growled.

Des stood, nose bleeding and lip split. He spit blood on the ground and smiled. "Is that so? Then I just thought of a suitable ending." Des grabbed my hand and turned it over. "If you refuse me, everyone you know will hear of your secret." With that, he placed a bloody kiss in my palm.

"What do you think you are doing?" Ryn growled at Des and snatched my hand.

"Now, she is mine." He enjoyed taking what his brother wanted. "This is much better than her just breaking you," he congratulated himself.

"What about when we return to school?"

"I don't care. I will have her either way."

I expected Des to let out an evil cackle or something of the like, but he just stood triumphantly, lording over our pained expressions.

"See you at the ball, my nymph." Des strutted down Main Street toward the inn. I felt nauseated.

"At least Reid and Ryn have declared their intentions as well and are allotted equal time," Flynn tried to console.

"But Flynn—" Reid began, looking hurt.

"Reid, no." Flynn shook his head.

"Flynn, that's enough." Reid lost his patience.

Flynn stared at Reid, astonished.

"I will not have it this way. I know you were content with helping me, but I can't be selfish any more. We will compete on equal terms and have no hard feelings," Reid declared with finality.

They stared at each other, silently finishing the

conversation. Finally, Flynn turned to me. Timidly, he took my hand.

"Ki-Ki," he said hopefully, pleading with his eyes. He dipped his head and sweetly kissed my palm where Des's blood was still smeared.

Warmth spread through my body, and I gasped. *Flynn...*Dumbstruck, it took a while for the gears in my head to start spinning again. I smiled my acknowledgment of Flynn's intentions.

Relieved, he released my hand.

I feel like a whirlwind has been tossing me around. I need to plant my feet. "You are in control," Dane had told me. He wasn't referring to this, but it still applies. I took stock of my situation. *Four men have declared their intentions toward me. At least three of them love me while the other is blackmailing me into consent to torture the other three. I can give up my dream and choose one or none of the three that love me; I can accept the one that is using me and pursue my dream; or, I can be clever and find another way.* Armed with a plan, I turned to the suitors gathered before me.

"I acknowledge each of your intentions and promise to consider each of you equally. I love you all as my friends but will see if that can blossom into something more. However, I will not be giving up on my quest when I am so close."

They all nodded in agreement.

"Unfortunately, that means I must also acknowledge Des. In this case, the rules of courtship are in our favor. You are all allotted equal time. He must relinquish my hand to one of you when his time is up. Try not to allow his taunting to affect you, and follow my lead. If he does not elicit the desired response, he may try another tactic or give up altogether."

"What about when we return to school?" Ryn asked.

"I don't plan on letting it continue that long. However, if he has not given up by then, I will address that new scenario." It felt good to take control of the situation.

They looked back at me with pride and determination.

While returning to the Nords' residence, we hammered out our plan of attack and the rotation of allotted time. Everyone agreed that order of declaration was fair, which meant Reid was first, followed by Ryn, Des, and Flynn.

Flynn did not mind going last as he would always get to snatch me from Des. Of course, then there was Dane, which could actually work in our favor. Des didn't know anything about Dane and, therefore, couldn't involve him. Also, Dane was my selected escort for the ball, so his allotted time was longer. The ball was in two days, so I had two days to prepare for battle.

You want to throw down the gauntlet on the field of courtship, Des? You don't know who you are messing with.

We collected Leif on the way to Sei's and told him what had happened. His mission, which he accepted, was to monitor Des's movements when he was not with me.

Taking my leave, I returned home. I begged

Mable for a snack since I had missed lunch. She gave me a meat pie she had saved for me. Locating Charlotte, I surprised her with my unusual request.

"Help me make a ball gown," I pleaded.

"But you have never been interested in clothes before. I guess finishing school is helping after all."

She gave me funds so I could go into town the following day with Patti to purchase fabric. The rest of the afternoon, I drew designs for a gown that flattered my body.

The next morning, I snuck out again to do physical training and was refreshed and ready before breakfast. I walked to the Nords' as early as was proper. Rather than tease James, I nodded to him politely as he showed me to the drawing room. Patti burst in, all excitement that I had, finally, taken an interest in fashion. I showed her my design.

She gasped, "So mature, Kai. Poor Charlie Jamison won't know what to do with himself."

Her coachman drove us to the fabric shop. After showing the owner, Jane, my design, she helped us pick a luscious red silk. As Jane cut and wrapped my fabric choice, I looked around the shop. On a shelf near the back of the store, I noticed a small charm in the shape of a heart. I recognized it immediately from my Magical Devices bookchip and purchased it with the fabric. Jane seemed surprised but didn't say anything about it.

Patti and I hurried home to work on the creation.

Charlotte was a true master at cloth manipulation. We mostly just helped her. It took her the rest of the day and into the next to complete the gown. It was finished just as it was time to get ready for the ball.

I had never worn such a confining dress, but after a while, I got used to it. Of course, it helped that Patti added a slit to each knee to help me walk.

Dane, Patti, and I were to meet Flynn, Reid, Leif, and Ryn outside the Jamisons'. When the time came, Dane appeared at my door to fetch me and Patti. Stella showed him to the sitting room. Patti went to him first, receiving the compliments due to a sister. At last, I presented myself to my escort. I did not receive the compliments that were my due, but I forgave him since he was slack-jawed and drooling.

Test: complete and successful.

Dane did not say a word or take his eyes off me as we left my house and he handed me into the carriage. Patti had to kick him in the shin to get an answer.

"Are you prepared for Charlie?" she repeated to her brother.

Horror struck Dane's face as he realized he was escorting me to a ballroom half-full of men and owned by Charles Jamison's family.

"You can count on me," he promised, determined.

We arrived at the Jamisons' after a short ride. Dane climbed out of the carriage, then helped Patti and me. Four handsome young men awaited us near the entrance.

Leif caressed Patti with compliments, and she blushed, pleased. Dane squinted at Reid, Ryn, and Flynn, but allowed them to greet me as suitors.

Their eyes sparkled, taking in my dress: sleeveless and form-fitting with a mandarin collar. Dane looked shamed as they complimented me smoothly.

Our party complete, we entered the Jamisons' large home.

CHAPTER 17

harles Jamison and his parents waited to greet their guests at the entrance. We all greeted his parents congenially; Flynn, Reid, Leif, and Ryn introduced themselves. They were overjoyed to have Leif Algren, and his friends, at their little party.

Charles Jamison took my hand in greeting. He bent over it as was appropriate but stripped my dress off with his eyes.

"Kai, did you not get my invitation to escort you?" he asked.

"Of course, I did, Mr. Jamison. Did you not get my response that I already had an escort?"

He looked at Dane as if just noticing him. "Dane, I guess you beat me to her. *Again.*" Charles stared Dane down.

Dane did not submit. "You should be quicker next year."

"Indeed." The line was piling up behind us, so

we were forced forward. "I expect a dance, Kai," he said as we walked away.

I shuddered unpleasantly.

The Jamisons' ballroom was magnificent. The grand staircase led us to a large glittering room with a crystal chandelier at the center. Though the Jamisons had blue shard-powered lights, their annual ball was always lit by candlelight. As the richest family in Sweet Water, they loved to flaunt their wealth. No one minded since they always made their events open to everyone.

Sitting me in a protected corner, Dane went to retrieve refreshments. With Patti next to me, I noticed Leif motioning the entrance from the refreshment table. Des slithered in. He spotted his brother first, who was keeping a respectful distance from me as it was Dane's time with me.

Des approached Ryn, not noticing me. I stood as Dane handed me a drink. Des must have asked where I was because Ryn nodded in my direction. He skimmed for me, going right past me. Then his eyes skipped back to land on me. His look of shock was satisfying. He sauntered in my direction.

Dane stopped him before he reached me. "Excuse me, I have precious little time with Ms. Stephenson tonight even though she chose *me* as her escort. Who are you?"

"Desmund Salvo, and I have stated my intentions."

"Ah, then where are you in the rotation?"

Des looked confused, and Dane turned to me, questioning.

"Mr. Salvo is after Mr. Breshire," I told Dane.

He nodded.

"Well then, Mr. Salvo. It appears you will have to return at your allotted time."

Dane is really enjoying this.

Des harrumphed and stomped off.

I guess he does not like the battlefield he chose.

The music started, and Dane led me in the first dance. He was not the best dancer, but we had been partners many times before. At the break, Charles approached to demand the next dance. Before Dane could respond, Reid appeared as if he had always been there.

"I am sorry, Mr. Jamison. I have declared my intentions. This is my allotted time." Reid took my hand and swept me away.

"Breathtaking does not begin to describe how you look, Kai,"

I flushed as he smiled knowingly. *You are* definitely *more dangerous than Flynn.*

Reid's dancing was proficient and characterized by his solid footing and strong grip while holding me. He reluctantly relinquished my hand to Ryn as the next song started.

Ryn danced smoothly, gliding me around the floor. His eyes and smile sparkled at me happily. "I hope you choose me. I love you no matter who you are." When the time came, Ryn diplomatically handed me to Des.

"You are a very sly woman," he said appreciatively.

"Well, I am full of surprises," I flirted with him heatedly.

Caught off-guard, he blinked at me. *I see you are not used to being chased.* I smiled, stunning him. Unfortunately, he did not take long to recover.

"I think I will have fun with you," he said, trying to intimidate me.

"Oh, I guarantee you will."

Our conversation continued like that for the rest of the dance, each of us fighting for the upper hand. Though it was a draw, it felt like a victory, having taken him off-guard quite a few times.

Flynn snatched my hand as the last note reverberated through the hall. Des was left alone on the dance floor, watching Flynn lead me away as the next song started. A quick look at Des showed his face was a war of emotions. Anger, confusion, and what appeared to be arousal. I felt a slight pang of guilt and squashed it ruthlessly.

Flynn's attentions soon had Des far from my mind. His expression poured out love, desire, admiration, and pride.

"Thank you for acknowledging my intentions, Ki-Ki. I'm sorry to add more pressure on you, but Reid is right. His chance of happiness with you was more important than my own. Will you forgive me?"

"You weren't exactly lying, Flynn. I know Reid is the most important to you."

He looked as though I didn't understand.

"You captured me the moment I saw you. To think any woman was that audacious! I had to know you. I became lost in you," he whispered in my ear, much like Reid had.

My knees buckled as a hot flash hit me. If Flynn hadn't stepped closer and caught me, I would have had an embarrassing fall.

"You ought to be more careful, Ki-Ki. I could get accustomed to this." Flynn smiled down at me as he held me to his chest. He led me to a balcony off the back of the ballroom.

"Do you remember when you told me about empathy?" he asked.

I nodded.

"I do not understand how you felt magical emotions, but I do understand empathy." His eyes bored into mine. "I see you. I know you. I feel what you feel, and I love you." He kissed my palm again.

My heart burst, feeling like it would bounce out of my chest. I stepped closer to him and wrapped my arms around his torso. Laying my head on his chest, I could hear his heart beating as loudly as mine.

"Flynn," I whispered, looking up at him. Everything I ever needed to say was expressed with me whispering his name.

He cupped my face with one hand and placed the other on the small of my back.

"I won't run from you again," he promised, dipping his head. His lips softly pressed against mine, waiting for my response. I moved my hands up his back and pressed my body to his. His hand on my back urged me closer, but his lips remained sweet and soft. They lingered on mine until I was begging for more. As insistent as I became, Flynn's patience was unbreakable. He kept the pace soft and slow.

Something yanked Flynn away from me. Cold and empty, I focused on Charles as he spun Flynn around to punch him. Flynn easily avoided the swing, and a gust of wind knocked Charles on his back. He scrambled to his feet.

"Charles, stop," I demanded.

"Don't talk to me with your filthy mouth, Whore," he spat at me.

In a flash of fury, I curled my hand into a fist and socked him right in the eye. "Don't you ever talk to me that way, Charles Jamison! I have been dealing with your improprieties for too long. I should have done that long ago," I berated him.

He looked up at me, shocked and frightened. Flynn looked impressed and grinned at me. We left Charles alone to collect himself.

The rest of the ball was a wash. I apologized to Mr. and Mrs. Jamison and advised them to put their son on a shorter leash.

While waiting for the carriage, Patti was grumpy. She had barely gotten to dance with Leif as he was too busy monitoring Des, and she had to distract Scarlet Winter most of the night.

Leif was contrite. "I wanted this evening to go much differently, Ms. Nord." He stepped closer to her and took her hand. Turning it over, he kissed her palm.

All propriety and upset forgotten, Patti squealed with joy and hugged Leif happily. She sighed and giggled the entire drive home.

Thanking Dane as I left the carriage, I went directly to my room. Lying on my bed in the dark, the night played before my eyes. *I am not sure my plan worked on Des.* It had all fallen apart in the end. Thinking of Charles' shocked expression, I stifled laughter.

I wonder if he will tell anyone I punched him or that he saw Flynn and me kissing.

That thought transported me back to the balcony where Flynn and I had clung to each other, and he kissed me sweetly but maddeningly slow. Then I thought about what we did the day we left school. I was glad I was alone to take care of the hot throb that took over.

The next morning glowed brightly, and I realized I had slept through physical training. I ate breakfast and went to Sei's. Four happy boys congratulated me on my performance the night before.

"I have never seen Des so worked up. I think your plan is working," Ryn said.

"I wish I could have seen you punch Charles Jamison...I am sure Roan would be proud," Leif grinned.

Reid asked if my hand was all right, and I assured him it was.

Flynn just grinned, but there was something telling in his eyes that stoked my inner fire. Our eyes locked, and the rest of the world fell away.

"I see," Reid said, disappointed.

"Oh, come on!" Ryn wailed.

I looked at them, confused at first. Flynn placed his hand reassuringly on my shoulder.

"You have made your choice. I am sorry it was not me, but I will still support you and continue to earn your friendship." Reid took my hand and kissed the back of it, withdrawing his intentions. He tried for a brave smile.

My heart ached at his pain.

Ryn followed Reid's sentiment reluctantly. "I can't say I am happy about this, but I respect your choice. I hope you will not be uncomfortable with friendship as I don't know what I would do without it," he said miserably, kissing the back of my hand.

I drew them both into a hug. "Thank you for understanding. You will never need a better friend than me." Wiping my tears, I got down to the problem at hand. "We still have the problem with Des. I am not sure if my plan worked or not. We will have to wait and see."

It seemed that being punched by a girl was not something Charles wanted to share because we heard nothing from our small community in the days that followed. The days passed easily. Sei drilled us all in physical training and worked with Flynn and me on air techniques.

Reid and Ryn's hearts were sore, but we were trying to find a new rhythm in our friendships. They were able to joke with Flynn about stealing me away if he messed up. Leif spent a lot of time at the Nords'.

After a week, with no sign of Des, I was starting to hope that maybe Ryn had been right.

One day, I heard Mable's whistle calling me home midmorning. Worried that something was wrong, I hurried home. Mable rushed me to the sitting room, where I found Des sipping tea with Charlotte.

"Kai my girl, there you are. This young gentleman has come to call on you. He tells me he has recently declared his intentions *and* danced with you at the Jamisons' ball?" Charlotte was not happy I had neglected to tell her this.

Covering my shock, I said, "Why, yes. How are you Mr. Salvo? I was not expecting you today." I gave him my hand in greeting.

"Not at all, Ms. Stephenson. I had intended this to be a surprise. Would you join me on a picnic today? It will be chaperoned, of course," he lied for Charlotte's benefit.

"I would be delighted," I said, convincing even him.

We left the house with Charlotte's blessing.

"I saw your handiwork after you left the ball," Des complimented as we walked arm-in-arm.

"I have no idea what you mean."

"I heard you yelling at Charles Jamison. Who else gave him that shiner?"

I preened and ignored his insinuation. "Where are we going?" I looked around for a picnic basket. None was in sight.

"It's a surprise."

We walked through the trees to the clearing and the spring that Toby had loved so much.

"The people in town recommended this place. And I thought, 'it sounds like just the right place for my little nymph.'"

I smiled at him prettily. "I love it."

My response to him kept throwing him off as he was expecting me to resist. Roan had taught me better than that: *"use your opponent's force and direction against him."*

He sat, trying to regain the upper hand.

"You and your brother really are alike," I commented.

Fury bubbled barely under the surface. "Did you just compare me to that son-of-a-groom?"

"Now, Mr. Salvo, do not be unkind. Ryn is my friend after all," I tut-tutted.

"Your friend? Not your *lover*?"

"My very dear friend, who incidentally, has recently retracted his intentions."

"He has?" Des looked unsure.

"Indeed, not a week ago."

Curiosity got the better of him. "Why do you say we are alike?"

"Well, he must have learned how to court from his older brother." I said it like a compliment. "Neither of you seem to care that others are seeing you with a man. Also, your approaches are similar."

"Our approaches?"

"Do you recall our intimate exchange in the library?"

He nodded.

"Well, I had a similar experience with Ryn at Jopin's. Of course, *he* was not interrupted. I dare say, *our* exchange could have ended similarly."

Off balance, he considered what I meant. "There is no one to interrupt us here," he said suggestively, moving closer.

Unconcerned and ignoring his suggestion, I continued, "Of course, you are fundamentally different in a very important way."

"How's that?" he said, ensnared.

"He loves you above all things. Despite your harsh treatment, he still loves you as his older brother."

I had cut to the heart of the matter, and the truth I spoke seeped in. Des sat quietly, looking unsure and lost.

"He feels the pain you feel and wants to ease it any way he can," I urged, placing my hand on his.

He looked up, surprised by my concerned touch.

"Let him in," I said.

"I don't know how," he whispered, defeated.

"I will help you."

CHAPTER 18

"Come on!" I pulled Des behind me toward Sei's house. He continued to drag his feet. *I never thought I would see the haughty Des so nervous.*

We broke through the trees into Sei's backyard. Everyone was outside, practicing or doing chores.

"I changed my mind." Des tried to make a break for the trees.

I refused to let go of his hand and kept him with me.

Our entrance caused silence to descend on the group. Everyone stared. I pushed Des in front of me toward Ryn. Des hunched, unsure and frightened. Then his default haughtiness started to slip back into place. Everyone else went on the defensive.

"Des, that's enough," I scolded. "Ryn, come here."

Ryn stepped forward, uncertain.

"Ryn, what did you tell me about Des at Peace Garden?"

He remained silent, embarrassed.

"Oh, for Heldan's sake! Just tell your brother what you told me."

Ryn stepped closer to Des and bent his head. "I am sorry, Brother." Long-restrained tears began to leak from his eyes. "I am sorry I was ever born. I am sorry our mother prefers me. I am sorry I could not make your home life joyful with unconditional love."

Des's anger and resentment were washed away by Ryn's tears. He placed both hands on Ryn's shoulders, and Ryn looked up at him, amazed. "Ryn, forgive your older brother. My envy is not something you should have had to bear." Des was clearly upset about the harm he had caused and finally understood the role of a sibling. They hugged fiercely as only brothers can.

"Tea?" Sei blurted, breaking the tension.

Everyone laughed and headed for the back door. Des hesitated to follow, but my encouraging smile reassured him.

Flynn turned to Des as we all drank tea. "So are you going to retract your intentions from Kai?"

"Why should I?"

Everyone tensed.

"I will not blackmail her into acknowledging my intentions, but I will not withdraw. She is, by far, the most worthy woman I have ever met. Will you acknowledge me, little nymph?"

"I have already chosen Flynn," I apologized.

"But that was before I was given a fair chance," he said, undeterred.

I glanced at Flynn, who shrugged.

"All right, I acknowledge your intentions, Desmund Salvo."

He turned to Flynn good-naturedly. "Don't let your guard down. I can be *very* charming."

"You're on." Flynn accepted his challenge.

The second week of break passed quickly, but we all had fun. I was surprised, but glad, at how fast Des fit in with us. When taking our leave, I promised to write Sei as did Leif in case I didn't. Our household staff was sad to see me go. My parents didn't notice.

After boarding the train, I changed back into my men's clothing and removed my wig. Leif begged the pleasure of joining our cabin to spend as much time with Patti as possible. Dane consented as long as he or I was present.

I smiled as I watched Patti and Leif adore each other. Dane's presence reminded me I had one semester to figure out how to create air. I tried to contemplate a solution during the three-day return to Capital, but his gaze was too much pressure.

We said our goodbyes to Patti, and Dane ensured she got back to school safely. Upon reaching Elemental Dorm and promising to meet for lunch, we all went to our respective rooms.

Climbing the stairs to the fourth floor, Flynn and I entered our block. Opening our door for me, he motioned me in, much like he had the first time. We quietly unpacked our suitcases. After I was finished, I walked over to his wardrobe as he hung up his shirts.

"Flynn." My sudden proximity made him jump and drop his shirt.

"Ki-Ki…" He held up his hands, warding me off.

I took his hand and kissed his palm.

"I love you, Flynn." I smiled at him, and he smiled adoringly in return. I took a step closer. "You won't run from me?"

"Uh, Ki-Ki…" The lump in his throat jumped as he swallowed.

I stalked toward him, and he retreated. His back against the wall, I purred, "You have nowhere to go, Mr. Williams."

I stepped within an inch of him, waiting for him to close the gap in consent. I could see him at war with himself, but desire won.

He reached for me, and we pressed together urgently. This time he did not slow me down. His hands stroked my back as his tongue flicked my lower lip. I moaned against his lips and plunged my hands into his dark hair.

Coming up for air, he lifted his head to take a breath. I trailed kisses and nibbles down his exposed throat, and he moaned his appreciation.

I needed more contact, so I ripped off his tie and unbuttoned his shirt. His well-toned chest and torso were exposed to me, and I stepped back a little to appreciate the view.

I trailed my fingertips down his abdomen to the edge of his trousers. That elicited a jump of anticipation from his manhood, which strained to escape his pants. I simpered at him, pleased.

Lust clouded his face.

"Flynn," I whispered. "This time, I want to help."

Taking control, Flynn spun me so my back was

against the wall, but he was still not as impatient as I was. He kissed me thoroughly, making me pant for relief. He trailed his lips along my jaw, and nipped my earlobe and neck as he unbuttoned my shirt. Unbinding my breasts, he worshiped the sight of them free.

Grasping my hips, he easily lifted me, and I wrapped my legs around his waist. He encircled me tightly in his arms and floated us to his bunk.

Laying me down, he sat up to imprint the sight in his mind. He trailed his fingertips over my smooth skin, making me whimper in need.

Experimentally, he rubbed his thumb over my nipple. My resulting gasp encouraged him. He dipped his head and popped my nipple into his mouth, rubbing the other with his thumb as if saying, "I have not forgotten you."

He gently sucked and flicked my nipple with his tongue. The pleasure kept mounting but did not peak as usual. The need was becoming unbearable.

Wanting to share, I trailed my hand down Flynn's torso again. Not stopping at the edge of his pants, I reached under the fabric and wrapped my fingers around his hard cock.

His eyes popped wide and rolled back as he moaned into my breast. A few tugs of the wrist and he was clutching my breasts, panting.

I smiled at him wickedly. Taking that as a challenge, he sat up, pulling the hard length out of reach. I started to protest, but his answering wicked smile made me curious. He unbuttoned and removed my pants, leaving my legs bare.

Kissing down my torso, he stopped at my core, where he peeled my underwear down my legs and removed them from one ankle. He bent my knees and spread my thighs, making me hold my breath in anticipation. Then he grinned at me mischievously.

I had always thought I would be embarrassed or nervous letting a man touch me, but I didn't have any of those feelings as I looked into Flynn's sparkling eyes. I trusted and loved him, and I knew he wouldn't hurt me. And as I felt his hot breath on my core, all that remained was the need.

Reaching under and around my bent legs, Flynn rubbed my nipples with both hands. I felt a wet flick near the top of my slit and flung my head back in pleasure. I gasped and my hips bucked, but he grabbed them to hold me in place. The light flicks of his tongue gave way to long deep licks.

Lifting my hips, his tongue dove deep inside me. My crescendo finally climaxed in shakes and sounds I didn't even know I could make.

Wet and relaxed, I welcomed Flynn's cock where his mouth had just been. The first few painful thrusts gave way to a totally different kind of pleasure.

Flynn slowly entered and exited me so as not to hurt me. We rocked in rhythm, moaning and shaking. Not long after, Flynn's thrusts became insistent. We peaked together as his cock pumped into my core.

He collapsed on my chest. Wrapping his arms around me, he buried his face there. I fell asleep, contentedly stroking his dark hair.

CHAPTER 19

A knock on the door made Flynn scramble out of bed as he threw a blanket over me. "Be right there!" he called to the knocker as he struggled to put pants on.

He cracked the door and peeked out. I heard Leif's voice say, "Did you fall asleep? You're going to miss lunch. Where's Kie?"

"Yeah, I fell asleep," he yawned convincingly. "I don't know where he is. Maybe he went to Peace Garden to work on figuring out his problem? I will go find him, and we will be right there."

I had to bite my lip to stop myself from laughing at his smooth lie. He closed the door and sighed, relieved. I climbed out of his bunk and stalked toward him.

"Who is this boy, Kie, you are looking for? Do you need my help finding him?"

"I don't know. I have never met the boy."

Standing barefoot and wearing only black trousers, Flynn looked like a mussed fae who had taken shelter from pursuers. I closed in on him, and he didn't resist.

"We should get dressed and go to lunch," he mumbled as I kissed his throat.

"We should," I agreed, trailing my lips on his collarbone.

The embers in my core started to heat again, and Flynn moaned as I pressed against him. "Wait. We really do have to go. We can't stay in here all day."

"Are you sure?"

"No, but I am pretending I am."

With effort, he put me at arm's length. "Later," he promised, kissing me on the top of the head.

"Fine," I grumped. I went to the bathroom and cleaned up. Upon exiting, I was fresh and ready to leave, but I was a little sore. Walking seemed to help. By the time we entered the dining room, I no longer walked like I was riding in a saddle.

I knew we were on good terms with Des, but it was still strange to see him sitting at our table. The students around us certainly had noticed; some openly stared. Sitting down with food, I reassured Des that it would pass.

He smiled warmly at my concern. "Thank you, little nymph."

I looked at Flynn to see his reaction. He looked secure and thoroughly unconcerned.

"Will you join me for a walk after lunch, my nymph? Classes start tomorrow, and that will give me less time with you."

Apparently, he was serious about courting me as a man even after I told him I already chose Flynn. The rules dictate that he is allotted time after I accept him until he either withdraws or dies, or I refuse him or get married to someone else.

"Very well," I agreed.

After lunch, Des and I embarked on our walk to nowhere in particular. He asked me questions about myself, and I answered honestly.

I told him about my mission to create air. I told him about Dane's deadline and how close I was to success.

"The part I can't figure out is how to feel my soul's frequency."

"It sounds like you already have," he mused.

I stopped abruptly. "What do you mean?"

"Well, normally, a fire user gauges magical frequency and then matches his soul's frequency. I know my soul's frequency by how I am feeling emotionally. Because you take the magic's emotion and feel what it feels through empathy, you have already matched your soul's frequency to the magic's."

I stared at him, dumbfounded. Eventually, I was able to ask, "But then, why can't I create air? What do you do after you match your soul's frequency to create fire?"

"That's actually the most difficult part, and it's different for everyone. How you visualize, what you think about, to create fire can be very personal. I remember the first time I discovered what fire was. I don't know how old I was, very young I would imagine. My mother had placed a candle on the table next to my bed. I was ill, and she was telling me a story. She told me about a little boy who followed a sprite through a shimmering door to Hest's hall. The flame of the candle seemed alive as she described the great fire at the center of Hest's hall. That's what I think about when I make fire, how alive that little flame looked to me then."

I watched him resurface from the memory and come back to the present.

"Do you have any strong memories of your connection with air?"

"Yes, but they are not pleasant like yours." I told him about Toby.

"Painful memories are not easily used for this purpose, but it has been known to work. It can also be destructive. Be careful if you are going to use that memory or find another."

"I will meditate on it."

"Perhaps you could ask Borus for guidance?" he suggested.

That seems logical. Why hadn't I thought of that? "Good idea, let's go to the shrine now. We have tons of time before dinner."

We walked to Student Hall and left campus by the main gate. There was a shrine to the Seven near the center of Capital, not far from the university. It looked similar to Gaami Temple with its triangular roof and columns, but Capital Shrine had inner walls to drown out the sounds of the city.

Inside the large chamber, there were eight altars. The one at the center of the room was the All Gods altar. There you could make offerings to all the gods, including the minor deities. The rest were along the walls, three on each side and one in the back. Each was dedicated to one of the Seven High Deities. Borus' altar was directly to the left of the entrance.

I dug into my trouser pockets and pulled out some coins. Placing them in the offering box, I grabbed a stick of incense.

On Borus' altar, there were lit candles and a container of sand. I lit my incense with a candle and put the stem into the sand to hold it erect.

"I make this offering to Borus, god of air; please bless me with the knowledge I need to complete my quest."

Sitting cross-legged on the stone floor, I emptied my mind. Nothing of import struck me, but I did feel more centered and calm as we left the shrine.

On the way back to campus, the streets were crowded with families on their way home for dinner. Two little girls skipped hand-in-hand, singing a song I knew.

I used to sing to Toby when he was upset. I would tell him that his blond curls and woodland eyes were signs he was a changeling. When he was upset, I would sing *The Changeling Boy* to make him feel better. I sang along with the little girls:

"Follow me, the fairy said,
Adventures we will have.
The little boy did go with her
To fairyland that night.
The morning glowed to find him gone.
His family, how they cried:

'Come home, dear boy, come home, come
    home.
Return to your warm bed.'
A changeling boy was placed instead
Into the boy's warm bed.
His family was overjoyed to have him back
    again.
One sister knew it was not him
And mourned her brother's loss.
Changeling boy made promises:
'Love me, as him, what fun we'll have.
I will not leave you so.'
Reluctantly, the girl agreed
And loved the changeling boy.
One day returned, the little boy,
A man grown tall and strong.
But changeling boy refused to leave
The sister he did love."

Teary-eyed, I finished the song and was surprised to see Des staring at me in awe.

"What? Do you not know that song? Is my singing that bad? Why are you staring at me like that?"

"You did it," he said in a barely audible whisper. "You made air."

I stared at him in disbelief. "What?"

"When you were singing, it was like no air I have ever breathed. It was fresh and sweet." He was so earnest that I had to believe him.

"I did it? I did it!" I squealed and hugged him, jumping up and down.

People in the street stared at the two men openly embracing in public. Des didn't seem to mind.

I grabbed his hand and ran back to campus. Charging him to collect Ryn, Reid, and Leif, I told him to bring them to Peace Garden. I sprinted upstairs to tell Flynn. Bursting into our room, I rushed at him. He was startled and tried to calm me down to tell him what had happened.

I dragged him toward Peace Garden, telling him along the way. Des had already assembled everyone else and updated them.

"First, I want to thank everyone for your help and support, especially you, Des. Without your help, I don't know that I would have ever figured it out."

They were so excited and demanded I show them immediately.

I planted my feet and opened my heart. Magic was feeling ...*wispy*... I let myself be carried away by the wispiness. Feeling light, I told the Magic: *I see you. I know you. I feel what you feel.* I took long breaths to match the frequency. *Sing with me, Magic.*

"Follow me, the fairy said..." This time I opened my eyes as I sang. A breeze lifted the hair from their faces. They breathed deeply and sighed.

Finishing the song, the breeze stopped. I thanked Magic and grounded my emotions. Then I let my joy fly as we filled Peace Garden with cheers.

"But, doesn't that mean you have to leave?" Leif asked, finally.

"Well, I did tell Dane that. However, I feel sharing this information is important, too. I will leave after that."

"Why not present it at the end-of-year festival?" Ryn suggested.

"Yeah, it's a cultural festival at the end of the second term where students perform and present to university alumni and donors," Des explained.

"That sounds perfect, and I will have all semester to prepare. But no one tell Dane just in case he doesn't agree. Let's make it a surprise, shall we?"

They all agreed.

We were rowdy at dinner. I am sure the rest of the students were wondering what was going on.

I was so wound up; I had too much energy to sleep. However, I willingly followed Flynn to our room. He wasted no time. No sooner was the door shut; he had my back pinned to it. It seemed to be a race to see who could unclothe the other faster.

"I am so proud of you," he panted into my ear as I kicked off my pants and underwear.

I jumped and wrapped my legs around him, kissing him from above. Grasping my bottom, hips, and upper thighs, he easily supported my weight.

I leaned my head back as he savaged my breasts with his mouth, licking and sucking my tight nipples.

My back to the wall, I slowly slid down his hips until his blunt tip spread my core. Completely encased, he shuddered and moaned.

Lifting me, his pulsing cock slid smoothly out of me. With controlled flexing of his arms, he repeatedly moved me up and down, in and out.

My arms clung to his shoulders, and I tilted his head up to crush his mouth with mine.

He brought me to release twice. I called on all the gods as I moaned, worshiping his name. When he finally gave himself relief, it was like an earthquake. His shuddering and pumping shook me.

He clutched me to him as I slid down his sweat-slicked body.

"Kai," he said reverently. He squeezed me tighter. "I don't want you to leave," his voice broke.

"I am not going anywhere."

"But what about Dane?"

"Everything has changed. Dane thought I couldn't do it, but I did. Everything will be different now," I promised, and hoped it was true.

He rocked me, fearing that change meant he would lose me.

"You said you wouldn't run from me? I will not run from you, either. We are in this together."

I felt him nod.

The slow strokes of my fingertips up and down his back soon had his cock stiffening for me again. "Now, let's try that again." I nipped his collarbone and pulled him toward my bunk.

He grinned at me, "I told you I would find your weakness and exploit it." He kissed me with heat.

I laughed at the memory as he settled on top of me. "Who would have thought my weakness would be you?" I whispered in his ear.

CHAPTER 20

The gong woke Flynn and me out of a satisfied sleep the next morning. I squeezed my eyes shut and cuddled closer to him. He had to drag me out of bed.

I had a new set of classes for the second term. Some were more advanced versions of the previous term, like Air Elemental II and Maintaining Peace of Mind. My history course was History 102: Building Terrenus. Instead of Magical Devices, I was to select an elective. I had been undecided until the day before. Luckily, there was still room in the class I needed. I opted for Music 151: Introduction to Voice.

After a quick lunch, it was time for me to meet Ichii at the usual place. I rushed to get there first. When he opened the door, I started my song without preamble.

"Follow me, the fairy said..."

As I sang and fresh air caressed his face, realization dawned on him. He glowed at me. "That's wonderful!" he praised once I had finished.

I mimicked his bright smile. "I can't thank you enough, Ichii."

"You really did it. Didn't you?" His astonishment was small compared to what the rest of the magical community was sure to exhibit. "How did you do it?"

I explained how the process worked, and he reacted similarly to how I had felt once the high of success had worn off a little: I should have figured it out sooner.

"I guess you don't need my help anymore," he said with pride rather than sadness.

"I do need your help for one more task, though."

"What's that?"

"Please do not tell anyone until I present at the end-of-year festival."

"It will be difficult keeping such an incredible discovery a secret for that long, but timing is every-thing, right? You can count on me."

I thanked him again, and we discontinued our meetings.

Leif and I met up with Roan soon after the semester started as well. Leif excitedly told Roan about me socking Charles Jamison.

"...and he dropped like a rock." Leif finished.

Roan nodded with approval. I sighed in relief that Leif had left out the part about how I had been kissing Flynn.

"But what did he say to you that you had to hit him?" Roan asked, not letting the point go.

"He tarnished my honor."

He nodded his understanding and didn't ask any further details. "While I am glad you are able to defend your honor, remember that it is just as important to know when not to use violence to deal with problems," he cautioned sagely.

I bowed my head to his wisdom, a little ashamed but not enough that I would have made a different choice.

After Leif and I sparred while Roan instructed, we exchanged schedule information. Our schedules still worked that Leif and I could meet with him three days a week before dinner.

My music master, Master Leelan, was a pompous man, frilly with self-importance. The class consisted of lectures on musical theory as well as private blocks of individual practice with Master Leelan. He didn't seem surprised by my higher singing voice and marked me down as an alto.

I had studied music with tutors before, but Master Leelan was on another level. He was strict and unforgiving. Even though most of the students in the class that semester were not music majors, he expected us all to view music as the heartbeats that kept us alive.

I was grateful my singing voice was decent, though that didn't stop him from cringing anytime I hit a flat note.

A few days into the new term, Dorm Leader announced that anyone wishing to present or perform at the cultural festival had to sign up soon. I rushed to the first-floor common area and was the first to write my name. I marked down that I would be singing, hoping that Master Leelan wouldn't scold me and say I was a disgrace to music by the end of the term.

I did write to Sei just like I'd promised. I told him our goal had been accomplished and invited him to the cultural festival. I also invited Patti as the festival encouraged discourse between Madame Bergot's and Capital University. I asked her for a special favor, which I was sure she would be thrilled to fulfill.

Though my time was quickly filled with classes, homework, sparring with Roan and Leif, and preparing my performance for the festival, it moved along in spurts. Some days felt like they flew by while others dragged on.

Master Tem was having a little too much fun during Maintaining Peace of Mind. Part of the curriculum was concentrating during distractions. He would walk around the circle and tap students on their heads or splash them with water; he even rang a gong in my ear. My singing was definitely off that day, to Master Leelan's dismay. I didn't even want to think about what was in store for the next class in the peace of mind series. Then I remembered I was not likely to be a student at the university the following year. That thought was far more distracting than Master Tem's gong.

I was still top of my Air Elemental class. Flynn didn't mind coming in second to me. In fact, he often rewarded me for my high marks.

Though I had figured out how to create air, I was still a beginner at the task. I spent many frustrated hours, away from spectators, trying to refine my skills in time for the festival. Those were the days that took the longest.

Flynn found me practicing one evening behind the dorm a few weeks after my discovery. After the twentieth failure, I growled and threw my hands in the air.

"I don't understand. Sometimes, it is so easy. And other times, it's impossible," I lamented.

Flynn looked sympathetic. "You just need to relax, Ki-Ki."

"There's no time for that."

An idea brightened his face. "Let's go." He tugged on my hand.

"Where are we going?"

"It's a surprise."

I followed him through campus and out the front gate. "Flynn, should we really leave campus? The dimming will be starting soon."

"Relax and follow me."

We walked to the trolley stop and caught a trolley heading east. I gave up trying to figure out where we were going and just enjoyed the ride and Flynn's company. The dimming was underway as we disembarked from the trolley onto a quiet street.

"Where are we?" I wondered.

"Wait."

I followed Flynn to a tea shop, which was closed for the night. We walked to the shop's side alley. At the back, a faint glow escaped the edges of a blanket hung on a clothesline across the alley. We crept down the alley, and Flynn lifted the blanket aside.

A street, aglow in candle and lamplight,

stretched before us. The sides were crowded with tents and tables with awnings. I gasped as I took in the colorful, dancing bazaar. People bustled through the small walkway at the center of the street. They laughed, ate, shopped, and haggled.

I stared in awe, and Flynn grinned at me. "I knew you would love it," he said with satisfaction.

He grabbed my hand and pulled me through the crowd. He didn't seem to mind holding my hand in public while I was dressed as a man. But, since it was to stay together in a crowd, it was probably acceptable. He pulled me to a food vendor.

"You must be hungry since we missed dinner," he guessed.

I nodded.

We ordered meat on a stick and stood to one side to eat.

After we inhaled our food, we explored the bazaar. There were so many beautiful things I had never seen. Clothes, jewelry, and knickknacks all seemed to sparkle in the flicker of the flames. A flash drew my attention to a copper bracelet.

Patti would love this, and her birthday is coming up.

I contemplated the purchase for a while and decided to buy it. My exchange with the vendor completed, I turned to Flynn and noticed he too carried a small brown paper bag. I raised my eyebrows at his bag, and he just smiled. We continued to explore all the little shops.

The crush of the crowd started to make me short of breath. Flynn noticed and pulled me down a dim side alley.

"Better?" he asked, facing me in the small space. I nodded, glad for cool, fresh air.

Flynn stepped closer to me and pulled a small object from his paper bag. Reaching toward me, he brushed the hair from my eyes and pinned it to one side. He smiled, admiring his gift. I felt the hair pin he had just put in my hair.

"Don't worry. It isn't too girly, so you can wear it anytime."

"Thank you." I beamed up at him.

A shuffle at the mouth of the alley drew our attention. There was a blur of a black blazer and a blue and white tie. We didn't see who it was before he was gone. My heart skipped a beat.

Did someone from school see us? Well, we weren't doing anything overtly sexual, so we should be all right.

"Don't worry." Flynn reassured me and squeezed my arm.

We didn't let a potential spectator dampen the rest of our night. We ate and shopped and watched the street performers without care. I was so tired on the way back to campus, but I was relaxed. I don't even remember walking back to the dorm, but I awoke there the next morning.

Des was very solicitous at breakfast about where we had gone the night before. When he found out, he demanded equal time. There was a bookstore not far from campus that he wanted to visit, so I agreed to accompany him. We walked there on a Saturday when we had some free time. He was looking for a new book by Robert Weller.

"Have you read his *Cave of Mist* series?" he asked, excited.

"No."

He proceeded to tell me all about it and how good it was.

The bookstore was set up like many others with shelves of drawers. This particular store specialized in fiction. We browsed the shelves, and I promised myself a new book once the semester was over. *Of course, if things don't go my way, I will have nothing but time to read whatever I want.* Thinking about what would happen after the festival depressed me, so I pushed my worries aside and tried to have fun with Des.

As we returned to campus, Des smiled with anticipation at his prize. We passed a small, deserted park, and I asked Des if he wanted to sit for a while. We sat silently, enjoying the wind in the trees. Finally, I turned to him seriously.

"Des," I started.

Looking at my serious expression, he nodded and sighed. "I know, my nymph. I was too late," he said wistfully.

"I'm sorry." I was sincere.

He etched my expression into his mind. "It may have been different," he envisioned.

I nodded. "Perhaps."

"Still, I thank you for allowing me to try to sway you."

The pain in his eyes made my heart sink, but he maintained a brave expression. *Any kind words from me now will break him.* I sat quietly.

He gave me one last longing look. "I do hope I will be awarded the same friendship you gave Reid and Ryn."

I shook my head, and he looked ready to crumble.

"You will be given a friendship all your own. It will not be the same as what I give Ryn and Reid just as theirs aren't the same."

He smiled gratefully.

As we returned to campus, I silently prayed to the Seven that one day soon Reid, Ryn, and Des would find the happiness that Flynn and I were blessed with.

CHAPTER 21

The attachment between Flynn and I was getting difficult to hide, or maybe it was the blurry figure from the bazaar. Either way, the other students had started to whisper. I didn't mind, but I worried about Flynn. One night, lying in my bunk, I asked him about it.

"Flynn?" I stroked his hair.

"Hmm?" he responded, listening to my heartbeat.

"Does it bother you that the other students think you are with a man?"

He lifted his head and met my eyes seriously. "I would rather them think I prefer men than them know you are a woman."

"But you didn't really answer my question."

He smiled. "No, I rather enjoy it. You are helping me pull off the biggest prank of my life. Just think of what they will look like when they find out!" He tittered evilly.

I relaxed. "You *would* think that."

"But what's all this? Does it bother *you?*"

"No, it kind of works in my favor. Like you said, if they think you like men, they don't know I am a woman."

"Do you miss being a woman in public?"

"Yes and no. On one hand, I am masculine for a woman and do not fit in to what is expected of me. But how I comfort or react to others can be very effeminate and, therefore, suspicious when I am dressed as a man. I think I will miss wearing pants. I know I will miss the freedom men are afforded. But at least I will get more attention from men when I return to my life as a woman," I teased.

"You greedy girl, am I not enough to satisfy your needs?" He mocked astonishment.

"I don't know..."

"I guess I have to prove myself." He smiled suggestively and trailed his lips down my body to make me beg him for mercy.

The term wore on and the cultural festival approached. We were soon past midterms, and Flynn was becoming uneasy as our potential parting neared. Not knowing what would happen myself, I tried to comfort and reassure him as best I could.

We tried to squeeze out every moment, even doing homework from bed. The only time we felt at ease was when we were in physical contact with each other. Our touching skin acted as a tether that reinforced our bond and made it feel like nothing could pull us apart.

I was amazed at how a full schedule and a looming deadline made time run away.

As the weeks slipped through my fingers, my relationships with Ryn, Reid, and Des became the friendships they should have always been. I felt guilty sometimes that my confusion at the beginning had led to them being hurt though I liked to think the experience had helped them grow. I knew it had helped me learn valuable lessons. I took solace in the knowledge that at least it had brought Des and Ryn together. The three of them were finally starting to look comfortable around me, without any wistful looks. I was even beginning to feel hopeful they might meet some nice girls at the festival.

The cultural festival was to take place over two days, a week before finals. The upperclassmen were particularly nervous as the festival acted as a recruiting ground for employers.

The day before the festival, I received a package from Patti. Opening it, I peeked inside and nodded with satisfaction. *Just what I asked for.*

My performance wasn't until the second day, so I could enjoy the first day of the festival with my friends. Some of the presentations and performances were serious, some merely for entertainment, and some were downright silly.

The entire campus was taken over with booths and stages.

I met Sei, as directed, by the front gate. Favored students were to escort their masters to an alumni mixer, which was held in the dining hall of Instructor Dorm.

I stood close to Sei as he chatted with old friends and acquaintances.

"Master Sei, it is an honor to meet you." Johnny held out his hand. "I have the privilege of instructing Mr. Stephenson in his air elemental courses."

I had never seen Johnny so formal and serious. I watched Sei in awe.

"I am sure you are taking great care of him, my boy." Sei slapped Johnny on the back.

"He really is a remarkable student. He learns quickly and far surpasses the others in his class."

Sei just nodded like Johnny was stating the obvious.

"Was there a special technique you used while teaching him?"

"The technique I used was on myself: question every preconception you hold, and do not be misled by appearances. See the student's potential as well as his current state," he advised wisely. "Be sure not to miss his performance tomorrow."

"I will be there," Johnny promised.

Many masters and alumni approached Sei. They all had equal reverence in their voices. Some that knew me complimented my hard work in class. The ones that didn't know me were intrigued by Sei's favorite student and practically begged to meet me. He told them all to come to my performance.

When the mixer was over, Sei released me to find my friends. Before I could locate any of them, I was found by Ms. Shale, and she was overjoyed to see me. Grabbing my arm, she insisted on helping me locate them.

Along the way, I spotted Roan. "Ms. Shale, may I present—"

"Roan," he interrupted, stepping forward and taking her hand. "Ms. Shale, was it?" His hulking size dwarfed her petite frame. She gazed up at him, enthralled.

As they stared at each other, I made my escape. "Okay. Well, good. See you later."

I found Leif and Patti on their way to see Ryn and Des in a duet performance. I joined them, hoping to find Flynn there.

Ryn and Des were performing on a stage set up in Fire Field, which was mostly a pit of sand. We found Flynn and Reid in the crowd around the stage. I stood next to Flynn and pressed our arms together, which was the closest we could usually get to holding hands in public.

The brothers entered the stage from opposite sides. They bowed to the crowd and turned to each other, taking fighting stances. Each ball of fire Des threw at Ryn hissed in a puff of steam as Ryn extinguished them with orbs of water.

A woman near us gasped nervously as their performance progressed. Upon closer inspection she bore a resemblance to them. I realized it must be their mother.

Their routine ended with Des soaked in water. Seeing us in the crowd, they headed our way, smiling triumphantly. Their mother intercepted them. She embraced Ryn tightly, kissing his face as Des watched, dejected. Then she turned to Des and smiled, placing her hand on his cheek. They exchanged words and embraced like they hadn't hugged in years.

She took Des's arm, and he escorted her off the field. Ryn told us they went to see the festival together. He seemed pleased and smiled after them.

We enjoyed the rest of the day to its fullest. We watched performances, played games, looked at art, and ate delicious food.

As the dimming started, Flynn and I returned to our room. Sprawled on his chest, we clung to each other.

"Tomorrow is the big day," I said unnecessarily.

"You will be wonderful," he reassured. "And, no matter what, I will be there."

The love we made that night was sweet and slow, like we had a lifetime.

My performance was to take place in Art Building as it had the best hall for music. Backstage, I waited for my turn to perform. Master Leelan bit his fingernails in the front row, worried my singing would bring him disgrace.

When the time finally came, I clutched the rubber balloon and walked out on stage. Shock fell on the audience when they beheld me in my green, shimmering gown. I did not wear a wig but styled my short hair with the pin Flynn had given me. Around my neck was my most precious possession, a sapphire-blue, satin ribbon.

Before shock gave way to outrage, I floated my inflated, tied balloon aloft and began to sing.

"Follow me, the fairy said..."

Because I had already communed with Magic before I went on stage, the balloon started to inflate more from the inside.

The crowd began to murmur as they realized what was happening. Their noise grew as my song went on, and the balloon got bigger. Sei stood in the front row and silenced them all with a level stare.

"...the sister he did love."

The balloon burst with a loud pop. Sweet fresh air and confetti descended on the crowd. I stood on stage and tried to gauge their responses. No one applauded.

Eventually, Flynn came out on stage and put his hand on my shoulder. He whispered in my ear, "Sei told us to meet him at the dean's office."

I curtsied to the audience and followed Flynn offstage. I thanked and released Magic as we left Art Building.

He threaded my hand through his as we walked to the instructor offices.

"You did beautifully, Ki-Ki." He smiled and patted my hand.

"Thank you." I walked closely to him, sheltering my shaken nerves.

The walk to the instructor offices was too short. We entered the building and heard Sei talking to the dean inside his office.

"You know as well as I that science as we know it has just been turned on its head, Glen," Sei argued.

"Yes, but what am I to do about it? A female has infiltrated my school. She posed as a boy, learned with them, ate with them, for gods' sakes, she even shared a *room* with one. What will her parents demand of me? What if other girls get that idea in their heads? The university will be overrun!"

"Glen, you are getting hysterical. She debunked an established scientific principle. One of *your* students discovered how to *make* air. Do you really want to give up this chance to learn from her?"

"Of course not, but..."

"Then say it was an experiment, a trial to see if a woman could handle this university. The Williams boy can say he agreed beforehand and was assigned as her roommate to protect and assist her. I will handle her parents."

"Oh, that *is* good. But won't other girls want to come here, too?"

"Indeed, they will. It is entirely up to you whether you give them the opportunity. If one girl could accomplish *all that* in *two semesters*, just *think* of what other qualified girls like her could do. And Glen, you are sure to get plenty of donors if you acknowledge and embrace the student that made this discovery."

"We are sure to lose some as well since she is a girl."

"But at least you will not lose your reputation."

"Very well, bring her to me."

Sei called Flynn and me into the office. Dean Cobb looked like he didn't know whether to congratulate or scold me.

"Well, dear girl, you have made a mess of things, haven't you?"

"Yes, Sir."

"I am assuming you heard all that?"

We nodded.

He stared at me sternly. "Do you still want to complete your time here at Capital University?"

"Yes, Sir."

"Very well, you will be expected to share your knowledge with the faculty, and you will be removed from Elemental Dorm immediately. Over break, we will erect a women's dorm. For the remainder of the term, you will stay in the vacant visiting master's cottage. We have a lot of work to do before the beginning of next term. You will also get your parents signed permission before returning. Is that clear?"

"Yes, Sir."

"Before you go, know this: it will not be an easy road for you. You will face much adversity. Keep your head up, and take heart in your accomplishments and abilities."

We were dismissed and told to move my belongings to the cottage. Sei stayed behind to refine the details of their new undertaking.

I was positively bombarded by people as we walked to Elemental Dorm. Their responses were everything from congratulations to threats.

"Be yourself," Flynn whispered to me.

I realized I had been cowering by his side as we encountered people. I straightened my spine and walked proudly. After all, I was triumphant. We barely had a moment's peace as people knocked on our door while I was packing. Flynn sent them away, telling them I would be out soon enough.

The visiting master's cottage was in-between

Instructor Dorm and Elemental Dorm. It was cozy and had a private bathroom.

"I want you to lock the door when you are alone. They will find out where you moved soon," Flynn warned.

I promised I would.

"I am happy you are not going too far though my bed will be cold without you."

The anxiety we had carried for weeks broke.

"That bed over there looks pretty cold; shall we warm it?"

He bent his knees and prowled toward me. I felt the urge to flee like prey. I didn't try very hard to get away, but I squealed and laughed as he flung me on the bed.

"I thought you weren't going to run?" He nuzzled my neck.

"It is in order to turn the predator into prey." I rolled and pinned him on his back.

He looked up at me. "It looks like I am caught in your trap."

"You are, but do you know how deeply?"

I slowly unbuttoned his shirt, kissing where the skin was exposed. He reached for me, but I kept his wrists pinned with a look.

When I got to the edge of his pants, I unbuttoned and freed his straining cock. Removing my underwear, I straddled his abdomen. My skirts sprawled out around dome. Holding myself on my knees, I inched him into my core, sheathing him.

He groaned and his hips started to buck. I stilled him by placing my palm on his chest.

Using my leg muscles, I controlled the rhythm. When I had milked him to our mutual satisfaction, I encouraged him to take control again. He showed me just how much it had cost him to keep his hands off me.

Dress ruined and completely satiated, I changed back into my school uniform before we headed outside.

Ha, I get to wear pants anyway, and I don't have to bind my breasts anymore. Win!

CHAPTER 22

The rest of the festival went as expected. Some people were impressed and asked me how I had done it. Others were downright hostile. Neither Ichii nor Roan looked at all surprised to find out I was a woman. I did get to meet Roan's sister, who laughed and clapped me on the back. I had no doubt she would be enrolling at Capital University the following year.

As the festival wound down, Sei found me. He wore such a look of pride. "I knew you could do it, my girl." He embraced me.

I gave him a letter chip to deliver to Charlotte. It explained everything and asked her not to tell my parents until I returned.

The next week was brutal. I slept alone in the cottage but ate at Elemental Dorm. The students had mixed reactions but most had come around. The air elemental students were particularly solicitous.

I think my instructors were harder on me during

my finals than they would have been a week before, but I passed in spite of them. Johnny was the only master who acted normally.

When break came, I looked for any reason not to go home.

"You are the smartest, bravest person I know. You can handle this, too." Flynn kissed me at the train station.

I shared a cabin with Patti and Dane, who would not stop flinging questions and apologies at me. Eventually, Patti had had enough and sent him to get refreshments.

Finally, I got to tell Patti about Flynn and me, and our time sharing a room. Rather than being shocked and berating me, Patti looked flustered and envious.

"I *wish* Leif and I could get time alone. I am practically dying over here!" she complained. "But aren't you worried about pregnancy?"

"No." I held out my wooden bracelet to her. A heart charm dangled from a small hole I had punched in the leather strap.

"What's that?"

"It's a rhythm regulator. I read about it in my Magical Devices bookchip. I bought it over break."

"But where did you get it?"

"Jane had them. I noticed it when we went to buy fabric for the Jamisons' ball."

"Why don't I know about this?"

"Can you imagine what would happen if all women were free to have premarital sex?"

"We'd all be less frustrated?"

I laughed. "I guess so."

Dane returned.

"I will show you once we get home if I can get away."

"Show her what?" Dane asked when he returned.

"Just an accessory at Jane's."

My dread increased the closer we got to Sweet Water. Every step toward my front door made me want to bolt. Bram was waiting to take me straight home when our train arrived. I promised to call on Patti when I could.

True to my request, Charlotte had not told my parents. I entered the study with a look of shame.

"I always knew you were an extraordinary child," Charlotte praised and embraced me.

"Charlotte, I am terribly sorry for lying to you."

"You should be," she said sternly. "And I won't make it easy for you in the future, Miss. Should your parents approve of you returning to that school, I will be taking the job of lady at the women's dorm."

I stifled a groan. *I will never be alone with Flynn again!*

Dinner was the time of reckoning. As we sat quietly, I cleared my throat. "Mother, Father, I would like your permission to go to school."

"I already signed to enroll you at that finishing school," my father said, annoyed.

"I want to attend Capital University."

"Are you daft, Girl? Capital University is a *men's* school."

"Not anymore." I told them everything, except

the parts about Flynn and me. As I related the past year, their expressions evolved.

My mother's distraction progressed to annoyed to shocked to proud. She absolutely glowed. "My daughter," she praised. "My reckless, brilliant girl, what I wouldn't have given to attend Capital University at your age. I might have been a *real* artist. Chase your dreams, my darling." She kissed me on the head.

I was dizzied by her surprising reaction. My father's response was far from encouraging. He was furious that I had spent all that time with men unchaperoned.

Still, my mother's praise wore him down, and eventually he smiled for the first time in years.

"Of *course*, she is brilliant. She is *my* daughter. You show those boys what it means to be a Stephenson!"

"Yes, Sir."

I was giddy with relief. We had a real conversation that night.

I awoke the next morning, fearing my parents' reactions had been a dream. At breakfast, they were both alert and engaged with plans for the future. A blissful week passed thus, and my parents remained actively involved with everyday life. While taking tea in the sitting room with my mother, Stella entered to announce a visitor.

"Mr. Williams," she proclaimed and showed Flynn into the room.

"Flynn, you're here." I rushed to embrace him.

"Kai, who is this young man?" My mother was,

rightfully, curious about whom her daughter clung to.

"Mother, this is Flynn Williams."

He bent over her hand.

"Mrs. Stephenson, I have stated my intentions," he clarified. "And Kai has acknowledged."

"Acknowledged but not accepted?" my mother wondered.

I stared at Flynn in horror. *I have not accepted!*

"Flynn, of course I accept your intentions," I blurted.

"I know you do, Ki-Ki." He smiled.

"Stella, go fetch Mr. Stephenson. I believe he is in the study with Charlotte," my mother said.

My father and Charlotte both answered my mother's summons.

"Mr. Stephenson, I am Flynn Williams. Your daughter has accepted my intentions."

My father seemed surprised but recovered quickly. "Do you also attend Capital University?"

"Yes, Sir."

"Good. I expect you to protect her while you both finish your degrees. Am I clear, Mr. Williams?"

"Yes, Sir." Flynn smiled and shook my father's hand.

"Stella! Tell Mable to cook up something special. My future son-in-law is staying for dinner."

AFTERWORD

Thank you for reading! I do so hope you enjoyed it. If you have a moment, I would very much appreciate a review on the store where you bought it. Tell other readers what you thought, and help them make a decision on this book.

If you'd like to stay updated on news about my books and events, you can subscribe to my newsletter on my website: www.dlieber.com

On my site, you will also find my blog, where I post all my fun little tidbits.

Thanks again! I hope you will travel through my worlds with me again in the future.

D. Lieber

ABOUT THE AUTHOR

D. Lieber has a wanderlust that would make a butterfly envious. When she isn't planning her next physical adventure, she's recklessly jumping from one fictional world to another. Her love of reading led her to earn a Bachelor's in English from Wright State University.

Beyond her skeptic and slightly pessimistic mind, Lieber wants to believe. She has been many places—from Canada to England, France to Italy, Germany to Russia—believing that a better world comes from putting a face on "other." She is a romantic idealist at heart, always fighting to keep her feet on the ground and her head in the clouds.

Lieber lives in Wisconsin with her husband (John) and cats (Yin and Nox).

Links

Website: www.dlieber.com
Goodreads: www.goodreads.com/dlieber
writing
Bookbub: www.bookbub.com/profile/d-lieber